EVERGLOW

Nandita Bose is the author of the novels *Tread Softly, The Perfume of Promise, If Walls Could Weep, Shadow and Soul,* and a collection of poems, *Dewed*. Her writing focuses on human relationships and hidden emotional lives of people like us. *Everglow* is her fifth novel.

She lives in Bangalore with three dogs, two cats and a food obsession.

EVERGLOW

Nandita Bose

Published by
Rupa Publications India Pvt. Ltd 2019
7/16, Ansari Road, Daryaganj
New Delhi 110002

Sales centres:
Allahabad Bengaluru Chennai
Hyderabad Jaipur Kathmandu
Kolkata Mumbai

Copyright © Nandita Bose 2019

This is a work of fiction. Names, characters, places and incidents are either the product of the author's imagination or are used fictitiously and any resemblance to any actual person, living or dead,
events or locales is entirely coincidental.

All rights reserved.

No part of this publication may be reproduced, transmitted, or stored in a retrieval system, in any form or by any means, electronic, mechanical, photocopying, recording or otherwise, without the prior permission of the publisher.

ISBN: 978-93-5333-551-9

First impression 2019

10 9 8 7 6 5 4 3 2 1

The moral right of the author has been asserted.

Printed by HT Media Ltd, Gr. Noida

This book is sold subject to the condition that it shall not, by way of trade or otherwise, be lent, resold, hired out, or otherwise circulated, without the publisher's prior consent, in any form of binding or cover other than that in which it is published.

To Rashi Kumar
The universe lies at your feet
when you sing the right notes

Contents

1. Rebel Yell — 1
2. Welcome to the Jungle — 8
3. Paradise City — 15
4. Living on a Prayer — 21
5. Highway to Hell — 28
6. Riding on the Wind — 36
7. Walking on the Moon — 45
8. Peaceful Easy Feeling — 51
9. Another One Bites the Dust — 58
10. Blinded by the Light — 65
11. A Whiter Shade of Pale — 72
12. Stairway to Heaven — 81
13. Leaving on a Jet Plane — 91
14. Creep — 101
15. The Boys are Back in Town — 109
16. Hello, I Love you, Won't You Tell Me Your Name? — 115
17. Knocking on Heaven's Door — 121

18. Black Magic Woman	130
19. Another Brick in the Wall	137
20. Helplessly Hoping	147
21. Rock You Like a Hurricane	154
22. Rock and Roll Ain't Noise Pollution	162
23. Bohemian Rhapsody	169
24. Free Fallin'	177
25. Here I Go Again	182
26. Every Rose Has Its Thorn	187
27. When the Music is Over	190
28. November Rain	197
29. Come As You Are	202
30. I'm Just a Singer in a Rock and Roll Band	211
31. Waiting for the Sun	218
32. Smoke on the Water	224
Acknowledgements	231

1

Rebel Yell

The weather changes. Circumstances alter. Relationships modify. Yet, I am in the same car, in the same seat. The route so familiar I could close my eyes and open them two minutes later to know exactly what I will see. The stray dogs I have visualized are there—the spotted ones that point to Dalmatian ancestry. I wish I could change. But an obstinate streak within me refuses.

From information that had trickled down to me, I know we are going to meet the director and crew of the proposed film. As is the norm these days, Sid volunteers no update on the drive out, the car stereo so loud it is barely legal. I cling to the distraction of heavy metal, only coming alive to my surroundings as we park at the edge of a forest-sized field. Late in the morning, there are knots of morning walkers, joggers, and in one shaded spot, a net-less volleyball match. The reassurance—if any needed—that life goes on as usual. Punctuality is a thing with Sid and we are the first to arrive though the director shows up soon after.

'This is Amit,' he introduces his ponytailed companion. 'With all our work, we collaborate. In reality, this biopic was his idea after your last Rock for All Concert.'

Amit who seems shy only manages half a smile. 'My knowledge of films, of most things actually, is merely theoretical. Param is being kind.'

I watch a football swerve and come to rest somewhere beside Sid. Hotly contested matches erupt often on the lawns at home. Rarely does he pass a football without being lured into dribbling for a bit. He passes the bright yellow ball to the players and swings back to the meeting, all adult.

Eager to take off, Param asks Sid, 'As a band, would you have any specifics on how you visualize this or how it ought to be presented? Any pointers for us?'

'To be honest, we haven't begun to think about the film yet,' Sid confesses. That is true. All of us are exhausted from the demands of gigs and the press lately. 'Perhaps we should make the best of whatever emerges as we brainstorm.'

A pause, and then Param turns to me.

'You, lady, are the X factor. Yours is a fable waiting to be told; an unknown classical singer, discovered by one of the greatest bands. You sing exquisitely. In a way, you extend the reach of Dreams' music and yet you engage in no other way. Even finding a picture of you online or offline is practically impossible.'

I meet his gaze square with a hint of a smile. 'Are you saying this just because I am a woman?'

Amit chooses to reply on Param's behalf. I notice their

thoughts overlap effortlessly. 'That is part of the mystique, yes.'

Bikes and cars join this informal conference. Finding myself a spot at the edge of a park bench, I let the melee unfold. For a while, the talk is mainly introductory, with the crew familiarizing itself with us—the band. In time, it settles. Discussion turns to details. In the glow of a sunlit mid-morning, it is easy to be swept away. The outline for the 'rockumentary' has outrageous specs. Its screenplay demands a narrative taut and precise, to evoke more curiosity than a mainstream movie. Apart from urban multiplexes, the large targets are diaspora and Dreams' fans across the globe. As Param speaks, his vision is contagious. The plan is to carve out a short documentary with the help of clever editing, later to be sold to television channels. It is also supposed to serve as a selling point in an exclusive DVD which is to hit the market as a collector's item after the launch. Within me, the dull apprehension has not yet translated to thrill at being on-screen. All along, I harbour the feeling that the one who stands here is not me.

In the lull following Param's presentation, informality takes over and conversations split within small groups until Amit assumes charge again. 'My question is for the band. Do each of you have a specific facet or quality that we could highlight?'

Yeah, like we are the Spice Girls!

Despite myself, I look around—assessing, assigning attributes. The stocky Vidyut who now sports a goatee is the ever-supportive ever-cheerful Mr Dependable. Endowed with almost morbid curiosity, Shady is our Live Wire. Ashraf has to be the Silent Knight, unconscious of just how deep an impact he makes on people by both his reticence and his genius. The tortured soul and angelic voice that combines in Nishith makes him our Wild Child. Then, my eyes stray towards Sid.

I am blank. When Sid appears, everyone—even the musical giants he considers his band of brothers—seem to pale. A quiet power radiates for he is at ease with himself. And it is visible in his tone, stance, aura, and his guitar. It is so easy to drown in all that sensuality. Except that ninety-nine thousand women feel exactly the same way I do, about Sid.

※

She comes in real late, sashaying up to us in the highest high heels. That red would have looked horrendous on most faces but not on hers and she knows it. Her hair is tied back with a delicate chiffon scarf perfectly matching the beaded cherry red of her outfit. She is not unaware she is making an entrance.

She throws herself in Param's arms and then half-turns to be introduced to us all. He obliges, smiling chivalrously. 'Juhi will be our anchor.' His eyes seek the approaching figure of the young gentleman who had come in her wake. 'And Zubin. A part of the film has been visualized as interviews to deepen the documentary feel and these latecomers are slated to do the honours.'

Zubin scowls, 'I had to wait for two hours in the car while madam here got ready.'

Her laugh is silvery dismissive. 'Tell Zoo not to get so negative all the time, it's soul-wearying.'

No one has noticed Sid until he returns, carrying a box. Wordlessly, he steps forward to where Juhi has just been deposited—out of Param's willing arms. With wet wipes, he sets about clearing all her make-up, almost messing her eyes with their streaks of mascara. A fresh tissue carefully wipes the lips clean. Before the awed gathering can react, Sid has, with a tug, let her tresses free, mussing them with his fingers. Pausing to survey his handiwork, he turns to Param.

'If she is to interview a rock band, this is the only way she can look. And her clothes simply cannot be this hideous pink!'

There is stunned silence. I steal a look at Juhi, almost a little outraged on her behalf. But her eyes twinkle in delight and the smile she strikes Sid with has an unmistakeable glint.

'I had been warned you are a horrible horrible man.'

Well, ninety-nine thousand and one now!

❧

On the way back, Sid suggests stopping for coffee. By now, I am both hungry and irritable. Outside, too many birds are singing of things I do not want to know. The offbeat cafe is almost deserted and we have the reassuring shade of the garden all to ourselves. He drops his question with the finesse of a bolt from the blue.

'How public do you think we should go about our love affair?'

'Excuse me?' my voice is more a polite squawk now.

For once, Sid looks a little uncomfortable—but not as uncomfortable as this is making me. Yet, his voice remains bland; as if this conversation is an extension of one of his business conferences.

'Through this rockumentary, a large chunk of our lives will be under close scrutiny. That bit I had not anticipated until the directors began to speak of interviews. I have no qualms saying it like it is. That may not be the same for a woman. Just wondered whether it would be better to come clean... Though, I am also open to keeping certain things private.'

There are times you can strangle a man, but instead, you sit, replying to his absurdity in the calmest voice.

'Firstly, what love affair? Just tell them you are engaged to Monica. And I can quite truthfully tell them I have never been involved with a man.'

His response is quick, as if he is required to do everything to defend the honour of the woman he loves—in a way, that makes me angrier. 'There is no question of dragging Monica into all of this. And honestly, Disha, it may have been ill-fated, short-lived and a bloody mistake, but it damn well did happen.'

My reply is stymied by the arrival of fragrant coffee mugs. I sit back stiffly while I am served. He takes a few deep sips while I just want to disengage from everything—this place, this topic, this irritant of a man.

It shocks me how bitter I sound. 'I am not the first young woman who lost her head and had sex with a dishy rock star. If you wish to specifically brag about it, you have my permission to do so.'

2

Welcome to the Jungle

Hope sank—the wild hope that the door was merely jammed and could be coaxed open. I began with gently jiggling the handle, until despair took over. I pitted all my strength against the door; it didn't work. Even when I flung myself against it until faintly bruised. When nothing helped, I thumped on the weathered wood, hoping someone would rescue me.

Is locking me out on the terrace another prank?

I pushed the thought away. It wouldn't do to add bitterness to the mix. Gradually, I accepted the situation. Night descended all around, until the air matched the colour of my mood. The neighbourhood wound down into the silence of routine.

A sound made me turn around. The door had opened, in a thin rectangle of light. But all I noticed was the figure it outlined. Perhaps it was relief at being rescued. Perhaps something about the lines of that silhouette did it. A powerful force seemed to take over, and it prompted a few hesitant steps towards the forbidding stranger. My movement alerted him.

'Who are you?' The voice was strong, harsh. 'And what are you doing on this terrace?'

There was authority almost arrogance in that voice and yet I felt drawn to it. Was I supposed to speak? In three long strides, the figure caught up with me. Strong fingers gripped my shoulders, bending to peer down at me in the light of an errant moon. The question was repeated, harsher. It must have been the moonlight.

His touch seared my skin. All my thoughts sought respite and comfort. And the soft cotton of his shirt seemed to promise that. And more. I needed that solace. I needed warmth, even if what radiated out of him was fire. Never had a man wrenched such a potent reaction in me. It gutted me. I tore myself from the jumble of those longings and his grasp, and hurried towards the door. He turned to watch me go. This magic demanded to be extended, if not explored. The only words I could muster were a low, 'thank you'.

I had trouble sleeping in this new household, just as the body refuses to relax in strange hotel rooms. And that night I had ample reason for the unease. Faint strumming of an acoustic guitar wafted through the drizzle and night air. With all traffic and human exertions stilled, my ears trained more easily on the music.

It surfed upon the moist night like a dream. The fingers were deft as a sitar player's; I could tell. The music was silken—serene and spellbinding. Then, the musician launched into an instrumental solo. There was something pristine, like crystal waters, in the sound. It harboured a mystery. And yes, there was a calling out, a wail, to its timbre. The bare melody was sketched masterfully, then reinterpreted, redefining the tune—which my music education later identified as the blues. Since the qualities of khayal are similar, a given format and then imaginative forays within limits, I tuned in with growing interest. It became a narrative without words. A story that unravelled without being told. I sat up to listen intently, drawn to this new dialect of music.

꩜

The first serious meeting takes place in Param's apartment. It is a small neat space with walls overrun by abstract art prints. White dominates the room. We are let in by his wife whose stiffness reeks of disapproval. By appearance, she reminds me of schoolteachers in the '70s—starched saree, thick-rimmed glasses, gimlet glare. We are told she is an executive secretary to a stockbroker. Perhaps, growing up, that gentleman had an affinity for teachers. She does make us marvellous ginger tea though, served with glucose biscuits. When she disappears through the curtained door to the bedroom, everyone seems to relax a little—everyone including Param.

Mild briefing intersperses our talk. When it comes to volunteering an opinion or speaking up as a representative of the band, even Sid holds back unless what is being proposed goes completely against the grain. Scripting had been entrusted to a knowledgeable rock historian, musicologist, and also a major Dreams fan, Shubhro. But neither is the script on schedule nor is the output of the quality Param had visualized. What irks him the most are the gaps he can still find.

Amit's suggestion seems sensible. 'I think a good way to kick off the interview thread would be with a focus on genesis. We don't need Shubhro to frame that. I guess we can brainstorm and come up with a set of questions ourselves. Like how the band came together and developed an identity, I mean, how you met each other and became this unit.'

Zubin turns to me, pale-eyed and solemn. 'I am most intrigued by how you came to be co-opted into all of this.'

⁕

Each soul has a travelogue. Mine maps out music as both the journey and the destination. Our home had always been rich in melody, just as open spaces are rich with oxygen. My mother and my two older sisters would hum or sing as they would go about their work. In addition, weekly informal music soirees were held at home. Only when I turned older did I understand how great as artistes some of the regulars were. Baba worked tirelessly to make sure that there were programmes in the community hall or the local places of worship so that everyone in the village had access to this form of celebration. If nothing else, soulful strains would waft out from small inexpensive transistors all around the house. Many evenings, Baba would relax by playing out recorded music from his prized stereo system as he pored over his work papers. Itinerant musicians, typically bhāts and bauls, stopped at our home, often knowing that there would always be a warm meal and genuine hospitality.

I don't recall when I first began singing. My formal tāleem began a little after my fifth birthday. Strange as it may sound, my Guruji started off with rāg Malkauns and not practice lessons in a Bilāwal thāt framework, that are prescribed. Far worse, I was kept to the two bandish I had been taught for over two years while all the others who had begun in the same class progressed through an array of delectable rāgs—Bhupāli, Yaman, Bhairav, Alhaiya Bilāwal, Kāfi, Behāg or Khamāj. I never gathered the courage to ask to be taught anything else. At home, alone on the terrace or the large gardens, I would try to replicate what I had heard the others sing. Perhaps Guruji was aware of it, for out of the blue, late one morning, he requested I sing a Mian ki Todi bandish. I blurted out the fact that he had not taught me that yet. And he replied nonchalantly, 'How does it matter? You know it by now, don't you?' Of course, the corollary to the story is that I was then stuck on Miyan ki Todi for the better part of the following year.

Though music is my prayer, I am also a strong believer of rituals. Old routines and habits provide a sense of continuity and ease in a new place. I tried to blend in, to hold on to what was familiar, as I struggled to make peace with my new life. My regular visits to the large ground-floor puja room offered just such a reassurance.

After my brief prayers in the puja room, I lit a bunch of

incense sticks and came up to the third floor as I did each evening. I normally encountered empty rooms. At the end of the wing I occupied, there were two interconnected rooms. One was a bedroom; apart from a narrow single bed and cotton curtains it was completely bare. Unlike the room it opened into, which was large, messy and forbidding. The implausible odds and ends included a complicated music system and speakers, a flat-screen TV mounted on a wall, other electronic gizmos, and five strange-looking guitars. There were books everywhere, towers of CD racks and many odd-shaped boxes lying around. This, I reckoned, was exactly how a housekeeper's nightmare looked.

I had finished my round with the incense in this room, still bemused at the chaos. I had barely stepped into the other bedroom when a voice made me jump out of my skin. It didn't help that the tone was furious. 'And what the hell do you think you are doing in my room?'

There was a figure sitting up from the heap of bedclothes. I froze. The gentleman reached out to switch on a light and glare at me—his gaze arrogant and beyond angry. That I knew by now who he was didn't help.

'If you ever step into this room or the next again without my permission, I'll lock you in and maybe a couple of years later someone will find your skeleton there.'

I hadn't missed that rasping edge of exasperation. It made me gulp.

'My name is Disha. I have come here to stay.'

'Well, Disha, stay in your room. Haven't you been taught

to stay out of strange men's bedrooms? And take that foul-smelling smoke with you.'

I looked at the incense sticks, miserable. 'It's a purifying ritual. It keeps the energies positive.' He looked about to snap. I hastened to clarify. 'I won't do it again. I was just telling you why.'

Sid fell back on the bed with his palm against his head. I noticed he didn't have a shirt on. His tone didn't have to urge me to scramble.

3

Paradise City

I am fascinated by windows. A city like Kolkata compromises with spaces. Endless seas of humankind sadly translate into an endless series of walls. Roads are narrow strips with walls on either side. The more beautiful a building or compound, the sturdier its walls. And I struggle to find ways past them. Windows are my allies. They let my eyes and spirit play in spaces I cannot. A sliver of the sky with streaks of translucent cloud shreds is enough. In the distance, the sun appears sulky-sleepy even when it is this late into the morning.

I don't know who started it. I think it was one of the twins. But all the young men in the household took turns to say it. They'd stop in front of me with a hand held against their heart and go, 'Dish...aaaahhh', delighted with this mangled version of my name.

None of them are flirting with me. They drip sophistication, and in no way can I possibly be of interest to such young men. The lifestyle I witness is cushioned by indulgence. Their days pass in lolling around at home in branded sportswear. In the evening, they dress spiffy and vanish in search of more fun—though how they differentiate that from work is a puzzle to me. It probably has to do with my response. I haven't known many men. I guess they sense I feel intimidated by their number and teasing.

In a household with a majority of young men, I had hoped Nina would be friendlier. But she rarely speaks to anybody, especially at mealtimes, which are the only times I see her. If she speaks at all, it is inaudibly to her older brother, Sid, who to the rest of us still remains quietly menacing.

I may have imagined it, but even the mob is slightly less unruly around him. The dynamics at mealtimes subtly changes too. The fearsome gang of six contributes to almost all the cacophony at the table. Yet, I've learnt a lot from their mostly inane chatter. From them I identify all those who live at home and some of their stories too.

That first rainy evening when I had arrived from Hamirpur with Amulya Uncle, I had been led to the dining hall and Aunty Parul had done the honours. The three young people with striking Caucasian features and colour I had guessed were Amulya Uncle's kids. We all knew his wife, Karen, was British. She had been the daughter of his English high-school teacher and Uncle had cut through impossible odds to marry her. These were the stories floating about when we were very young.

And there were simply too many similar-looking young men.

'We have individual personalities and prefer to be treated as individuals,' one of them had told me solemnly. 'And the first mark of respect from a guest is that you recognize each of us. As individuals.'

I'd sat blinking, not even half of the strange-sounding names had registered. Then everybody had burst out laughing.

'Don't tease Disha,' Aunty Parul had scolded. 'She has just travelled a long way in this awful weather.'

When Amulya Uncle had joined the rest at the table, he had sounded mildly reassuring. 'So have you met everybody? Don't let the boys intimidate you. They are terrible. But I hold their allowances in my hands, and one step out of line means they'll have to pay for it, literally.'

His smile had been teasing but meaningful, as he'd looked around the table.

'That's not how you speak about your family to outsiders, Dad. We are great guys and you know it.'

'Disha is no outsider, Joe. From this evening, she is a member of this family and I hope you understand what that means. When you lot gang up, you are an irresponsible, rowdy mob. And I won't have you bullying Disha.'

And so I knew that red-headed hulk who seemed the epicentre of trouble was Joe. Yet, in a way, I was thankful for all their blabber and the information they managed to convey about this mildly daunting new household I had come to occupy.

Another factoid I'd picked along the way was that the two rooms beside mine were technically Jimmy's and Dave's.

When Tony had been bumped up to a suite after his wedding, Joe had somehow hustled his room, which was not only spacious with an expansive bed but also equipped with the best AC. That persuaded both J and D to bunk in with him and they only came to their rooms once in a while to change or to work off a passing spell of heartbreak.

I knew from their gossip that Sid played lead guitar for a rock band even I had heard of. Anyone who spoke Bangla and was even fleetingly interested in music would have. Derozio Dreams has that reputation and beyond—a massive fanatic following. If I needed another reason to be further disconcerted by him, the fact he was a celebrity whose photos were plastered across newspapers and magazines was probably it.

❧

The Banerjee residence is sprawling. It stands among the quieter lanes of a green Kolkata suburb, a segment where the ubiquitous apartment blocks have still not made their foray, and homes—even the very old ones—stand largely retaining their past glory despite the ravages of time and potent Kolkata monsoons. Among these moneyed neighbours, this house seems a fraction more opulent and self-assured.

The façade, with its sconces and scrolls, whispers of generous proportions. And the elegant building with the vast green lawns and the spacious red-tiled sheds of the garage at the side is an oasis of old-world luxurious living. The insides are at odds with the exterior's apparent promise of romance from the bygone times. The decor has been remodelled smart, furnished in unusual bright hues of mainly greens and blues, in a practical contemporary style.

If nothing else, just the comings and goings of this overpopulated household were kaleidoscopic. As complex as the ebb and flow of the unfathomed deep. That the right amounts of food appeared at mealtimes was a triumph, owed mostly to Aunty Parul's prowess at managing the kitchen. My mind boggled at it all. I was also puzzled at how many diverse requirements, hobbies, leisure and social activities drew the family in and out of the massive iron gates all day.

I had run into Sid by the strangest coincidence of him being my guardian's son. But despite the brief intersection of all our worlds at mealtimes, I mostly kept to myself. That is how I would have liked it to be. That he was also a star and demonstrated it via his demeanour helped in keeping to my resolve. He, however, seemed predisposed to treating me with greater warmth that was as enervating as annoying.

Prayer has been an integral part of my life. But I have never needed its support more than I did that evening. Though most of the common areas of the house have generator backup, the puja room doesn't. When the power cut plunged the immense hall into an eerie darkness, I continued with my prayers, along with ringing the small brass bell, trying not to be uneasy.

'Shall I bring you an emergency light?'

The voice was familiar by now. It was one of the very few that engaged with me as a person.

'I'm done. Besides, there are all these oil lamps.'

He turned to leave while Jimmy, who had barely stepped into the room, was already out.

'Would you hold on for a moment, please?'

Jimmy's head ducked in now, oozing curiosity.

'It's just that Ranjan Uncle had brought these sweets to be offered to the gods this evening.'

He waited till I walked up with my small tray of offerings. The enticement of goodies had drawn Jimmy right back in—all the cousins are virtual caterpillars. He helped himself to a happy fistful though Sid carefully picked only one, which he then broke into two and ate just one half. Then, he held out the other half to me.

'If anything further is to be done, I'd strongly advise the emergency lights.'

'I'm done now. You can carry on.'

'There's nowhere in particular to go. Jimmy and I have just come back from office.'

Ever-enterprising, Jimmy seized the opportunity. 'And we're famished too. See if you could organize some tea, Disha.'

'Disha somehow seems to take on a whole lot of stupid work around the house as it is. The last thing she needs to do is make sure you lot eat even more. Organize your bloody tea yourself,' Sid cut in curtly.

4

Living on a Prayer

The third floor emptied out completely on most evenings. Often, I would go to the library downstairs to pick up books that I read in the privacy of my room. I had always enjoyed reading but seldom had the leisure earlier. Now, I spent my happiest hours curled up with books.

The only unread book in the latest lot failed to grip me. There seemed a strange hollowness within. I found myself sitting cross-legged on the white flowered rug that lay on the other side of the bed, next to the white dresser.

It was a rather leisurely rendition of Rāg Bāgeshri, which used to be Baba's favourite. Thoughts of Baba tinged my music and made it more beautiful, poignant somehow. My throat felt heavier, husky with memories. I had been enrapt in the music. And it was with an icy numbness that I became aware of a shadowy figure leaning against the latticed frame at the foot of the bed.

'Why did you stop?'

The voice was Sid's. I felt only slightly reassured it wasn't a marauding intruder, but I couldn't resume singing.

'You aren't supposed to be in my room either,' I decided to point out.

'Every musician needs an audience. I thought you needed a tānpura for that. Why didn't you bring it along?'

I wished to neither speak nor sing. 'I didn't think I'd be singing.'

∽

Lunchtime seemed to come too early. The talk had been frenzied and ceaseless. I actually felt a pang of sympathy for Mrs Param, trying desperately to keep at her work-from-home routine above the buzz of it all. We were here too often and it didn't escape me that it was a fairly unforgiveable intrusion.

Hungry hard-working hordes have to be fed, as all good generals know. For a while, all higher philosophy was bypassed for the most fundamental one: good food. There was much discussion over tattered menu lists encased with care in a clear plastic cover. I was asked for preferences. I had none but had a tough time convincing people that. Soon, a small feast, roughly enough to feed a small village, was decided upon. And so, Amit dialled a trusted nearby takeaway for the much-needed sustenance.

When the lady of the house finally emerged from their bedroom, her frown revealed she'd expected all of us to have long gone by then. Param went to the kitchen for what seemed an emergency conference and didn't seem to have a happy outcome. In a while, she came back and plonked a stack of newspapers, paper plates, disposable glasses and steel cutlery with considerable annoyance before retreating to the bedroom again. While I felt mortified at taxing the limits of this household, no one else seemed the least bit perturbed. The film discussion had been scintillating.

※

The occasion was such that it had called for venturing out of my room. The air all around had been, for a while now, heavy with the excitement of the Durga Puja festivities. And now, on Maha Ashtami, it seemed to have reached a crescendo even I could not remain unaffected by as stray bits of this phenomenon impinged on my solitude—increased traffic, bustle on the streets, the raw throb of the dhāk. Not that I did anything adventurous. I just took a book to the sit-out outside my room, sat on the floor and tried to immerse myself in its fictional world. The household, I knew from the past two days, had other concerns. Not that I wished I had them too. Occasions like these contrasted starkly with my past, underlining my unease in these surroundings—my alienation.

'Haven't you gone out?'

Dishevelled and sleepy, Sid looked as if he'd just woken up as he called out from his end of the sit-out. I stole a look at my watch. It was past noon. He came up to me now.

'Go, get dressed. Let's go see the neighbourhood deity.'

'I don't have Durga Puja this year. I mean, I can't celebrate. Because of Baba's demise.'

'Don't look at it as a celebration or even a ritual. Just an outing. Sightseeing, if you like. An experience of this city at its most bewitching.'

'I'm fine, thanks.'

I may as well not have spoken.

'Ten minutes, then.'

And he rapped on my door down to the precise last second. The venue of the puja was just two roads down, he informed me. Pure joy wafting in the air whose only expression was celebration. Vendors lined the pavements on both sides with ice cream carts, puchkas, spicy egg rolls, balloons and toys. The actual venue where the deities were had fewer people chit-chatting among scattered groups of chairs.

'Sid! Found time at last.'

Sid turned to greet the gentleman flashing a huge organizer badge.

'I was in Mumbai for a couple of days, took an early morning flight in.'

The guy stood alongside, while Sid refused to read the puzzled glances thrown at me. Suited me; I preferred the anonymity.

'We've organized a lavish lunch this afternoon. Don't go without any.'

He flagged down a young man who wore a similar badge, only smaller.

'Amol, I am giving you the responsibility to take care of Sid and errr...his guest.' He looked hopefully at Sid but his still gurgling curiosity was given no respite. 'Make sure they have lunch. Make sure they find a seat under the fans, you understand?'

I hadn't budgeted for this. And now, we were being ushered into a large tent and to comfortable seating. While we sat, a steady stream of people came over to meet their local hero, Sid. I could sense that we were being given special treatment because a fair number of volunteers hovered around fussing and beaming. Until I'd done justice to all that was set before me I hadn't realized I was hungry. Somehow, Sid joined in with the combined efforts to make me eat even more.

'Some chutney then to round off the meal? And if you won't finish your potatoes, may I have them?'

Before I could voice my dismay at him eating from my plate, he'd helped himself. Then, Sid proceeded to ask for two helpings of everything while I sat beside him, equally horrified at how much he could eat and the speculative glances now being thrown my way. It was not just that I was a stranger in these parts, but that I was with Sid and he was demonstrating this unwarranted ease with me.

After Sid was finally done, someone ran up to offer us paan. A large group of gentlemen, all flashing their badges, sat in a circle on red plastic tent-house chairs. Someone came up to pin a similar badge onto Sid's almost disreputably faded T-shirt as another rose to offer us chairs.

'Your band ought to have played for one of our evening shows. You are from our neighbourhood.'

'You think, Shekhar, we haven't approached Sid before? Never complies, though.'

Sid smiled as if he had been in sticky situations like this before and knew much about the right things to say. 'Any time you guys want. No issues at all. Musicians perpetually crave performance opportunities, Naren-da, but not during festivities. Quite honestly, Pujo and rock don't mix. I feel they shouldn't be forced to either.'

'You know, Sid, what kind of shows happen all over—from schoolgirls doing risqué item numbers to boudis shaking their booty to Rihanna. Rock is tame, almost prayer, by comparison.'

'What others do, Shekhar, I cannot comment on. But given the irreligious, almost irreverent nature of our music, I don't think it is appropriate for the occasion of Pujo. Call us after Lokkhi Pujo and we'll give you our best show ever.'

'There are some things I wish you could understand, Sid. There is fierce competition between rival Pujo organizers. It is complicated—matters of funding and sponsorship and all, too. And hosting a Dreams show would be a major coup for all of us; it would make the cash inflow so much happier.'

Sid turned, still smiling, and called out, 'Shobhon, please bring your mike over.'

The volunteer, who had been intermittently making announcements regarding the evening's schedules and lunch arrangements, hurried across. Sid now spoke into it with ease, almost conversationally. 'This then is my peace offering. I'll present you guys with the rarest of rare offerings, a performance by my guest, the talented Disha Ray Chaudhury, whose forte is devotional music.'

The stunned outrage almost wouldn't let me take the mike. But I did. I had never refused to sing at any temple or religious ceremony before and not all of Sid's stupidity would induce me to make an exception now. Both the songs I sang were addressed to Goddess Durga. The format of the first was more of a musical narrative in everyday Bangla, a concise version of the battle from the Devi Mahatmiya. In fact, I had to undertake the second when the enthusiastic applause and cries of 'once more' refused to die down. I chose a simple celebration of Her many forms in a unique version of Rāg Durga where the taboo nishād is incorporated in its komal form without altering the melodic integrity of the base rāg.

On the walk home, only after Sid had downed umpteen cups of tea as he hung around socializing lazily all afternoon, I ventured to break the silence.

'How were you so sure I sing any devotional music at all? What if I didn't?'

His sandal-shod feet slowed down as he turned to answer.

'I know you, Disha. Besides, I only need to hear the first five notes out of any musician to gauge their repertoire.'

5
Highway to Hell

At late morning tea break, Shady was being indiscreet and, well, shady again.

'Nishith was the most stuck-up bastard at St. A's and considering that school is crawling with only stuck-up bitches and punks, he was simply the most obnoxious prick in this heady city at that time. Any room kind of stank up when he walked in.'

Nishith blew him a kiss. 'I love you too, bro!'

'I swear to god, every word I speak is true. You were insufferable! Wait a minute. Am I sure I can say that in past tense?'

Being who he is, Shady was only mildly aware of the unease of his audience at this point. To his credit, he was mildly aware and he decided he needed backup.

'Ask Vidyut, if you don't believe me.'

And that put Vidyut in a spot for though he is painfully a stickler for the truth, so help him god, he could not really be as indiscreet as Shady. He chose a waffled bypass.

'The rest of us all knew each other. That way, Nishith was new.'

The way he said 'new' was loaded. Uncharacteristically, Ashraf came to the rescue. 'I don't care. I didn't care then and not now either.'

Now Ashraf spoke firmly, and actually faced the room as he spoke. For many, this was perhaps the first time they'd heard his voice.

'When we decided to formalize the college band, a roomful of lead singer aspirants showed up, most of them giving us headaches. There was this guy who just sat way at the back of the room, smoking non-stop. We thought he was hanging around only because he thought it was cool. At almost eight in the evening, just as we had given up and begun pack-up for the night, said silent smoker took the mike. Nishith has the voice of an angel. He is our lead. That is all that matters.'

'Thanks, man!' Though Nishith spoke nonchalantly, the tone tipped me off he wasn't as unperturbed by Shady's words as he made it out to be.

All of us returned to our cups of tea. However, discussions once begun seem to have this propensity of ballooning.

'So far, Disha, you've told us about Sid hearing you while you were practising and that one time he coerced you into singing at the neighbourhood Durga Puja celebrations. Did you practise regularly all through? Did Sid and you discuss music sometimes? And, confess, did you not hope Sid would offer you something more substantial musically?'

At mealtimes, I stuck with my policy of not speaking until I was spoken to. It was normally a polite question by the elders or a tricky one posed by the gang in the event of an internal dispute, where any answer would land me in hot water. It was only Sid who ever began meaningful conversations with me. Yet, at the table, he remained remote, even more of a stranger than any of the others.

I was taken by surprise when, just as we were winding up lunch, he chose to address me. 'Meet me at the gates in about fifteen minutes, Disha. I need to take you some place.'

His mother looked at him, seeming surprised and not pleasantly. 'Why do you want to take her somewhere? Where do you want to take her?'

Aunty Karen had taken to referring to me as 'she' or 'her', never using my name. All eyes at the table swivelled to me now. Sid's eyes narrowed.

'I have no clue what you're saying, Ma. Would you have a problem coming out with me, Disha?'

Not sure where all this was coming from nor how to answer him, I was relieved when Amulya Uncle came to my rescue. 'I think it is a good idea, Sid. I don't think Disha leaves home at all, except for errands.'

'We need to leave around 1:45. Be ready by then.'

A guitar was strapped to the back seat of the SUV Sid drove. By nature, Sid is quiet; that much I know by now. The only time he spoke was into the hands-free kit, and from what I could gauge, those were all work calls. I was left to introduce myself to Kolkata by looking at the buildings flit past and by reading street names off the shop hoardings.

Our destination was another sleepy residential area—quiet, green, with sprawling homes hidden away. As Sid parted the gates, three molten brown cannonballs flung at him—happy adorable spaniels. Sid knelt amidst the ecstatic wagging of tails and many licks and nicks of delight and introduced me to Cookie, Muffin and Brownie.

'My friend, Vidyut, loves his sugary snacks.'

Vidyut was smiling, and sweet himself, his fondness for dessert obvious from his heavier build. He seemed sturdy and dependable, like a rock. There was another thin-faced intense young man I was introduced to—Nishith.

This wood-floored cavern of a room had a large gleaming drum kit at the far end. Guitars leaned against walls and wires criss-crossed all over the floor. In a while, two more guys came in. All of them greeted each other with hugs, epithets and teasing, a kind of quieter warmth and ease that I had not known existed among men. Or perhaps I was scarred by the rowdy six at home.

These two were Ashraf and Shady; the latter name coined from two halves of Shailesh Dey. Shady was the cute talkative one who was shushed the most. He looked me over appreciatively before turning to Sid with a teasing smile.

'And I was told all along there was a strict no-girls policy here.'

'Disha is kind of like a sister.'

He got me a chair then before going back to ignoring me completely. Ashraf unpacked, tinkered around with wires and plugs and went plink-plink on his keyboard till he was satisfied with the testing. What he played seemed simple but well-integrated syllables of sound. I recognized them. It was exactly the same contour I took on the rare occasions I ventured into composing—a catchy cluster of notes that wouldn't quieten in the head. Shady, who played bass, provided the rhythm accompaniment when Ashraf repeated the basic framework.

'Great. Let's do a piece around it,' Sid suggested. 'We'll all work to fix the lyrics. Perhaps we can revive the Ichhamati song.'

Still talking and lapsing into jokes I didn't quite understand, one by one, everyone took their places. My exposure to rock music was woefully inadequate, just the tired old stale stuff I'd heard floating about as a schoolgirl. Yet, I could tell all of them sounded extremely good. It perhaps had a lot to do with the inherent musicality in what and how they played. Or the synergy they created in their compositions. Their music had spaces where each person could showcase what they did and portions where all of them played in unison, orchestrating in harmony. Every bit of it seemed so fine-tuned, so effortlessly perfect. Pure music drenched me through like joy. I leaned forward to hear better, to pick up nuances I didn't know, and it was with a dawning comprehension that this session I was privy to was indeed a rare privilege.

During break a lot later, Nishith glugged down half the contents of a bottle of water and lay on the floor—his forearms over his eyes, seeming exhausted. The others seemed a lot less tired and stood around chatting while Vidyut organized tea and snacks. It was all relaxed until Sid went and got Nishith's mike to me.

'So now it's your turn; sing something.'

I was horrified.

He was making a damn habit of it!

And their music, though beautiful, had been so alien it befuddled my mind. My only defence was a glare. Bounced right off his thick skin.

'You could sing some of that rāg from that evening,' he prompted.

'I can't. It doesn't come that way.'

'You are a musician, Disha. It should come every which way.'

All the eyes in the room were on me now. I took a deep breath, now mad at Sid, and preparing to refuse firmly. He couldn't do this to me all the time. But I found myself singing instead. Initially, my voice sounded unsure, heavy, fuzzy, but in a moment or two, I was elaborating on the rāg framework with practised ease. The rishabh and the pancham are to be used only indirectly, in specific combinations, and most of the guys in the room seemed to appreciate the ebb and flow of this unfamiliar music—I didn't try to guess whether it was knowledge or instinct.

There was silence when I stopped, having explored at the furthest reaches of my scale at the higher octave before returning to my home base of the familiar shadaj.

'Do you know a folk song?'

It was Sid again.

I thought for a while before speaking, 'I haven't sung this in a while so the lyrics may be a bit garbled.'

I sang a bhātiyāli—a Bangla boatman's song—melodic and solemn, recalling vast expanses of the River Padma and the wholesome communion with god its beauty mediated.

Vidyut commented appreciatively, breaking the silence that followed. 'What a great voice, Sid.'

Ashraf reached out to his keyboard and played out that piece again, asking me to sing along as he parsed it into small easy fragments. He'd keyed in something and now what cascaded out of his synth were the mellow notes of a piano. Nishith came to stand beside me and as we sang together effortlessly, I couldn't help but marvel at the quality of his voice and the sheer power of his lungs. Interactions with male singers are not new so I adjusted to the scale differences almost instinctively. I used the supple sounds of vowels in an ālāp form while Nishith used musical scat to sketch out the tune. We sang, enjoying the freedom of unbound sound, accompanied by the nimble magic of Ashraf's fingers. That done, the band went back to practice again. This time I felt drawn to the music, almost developing a kinship with everyone who had played with me.

I found myself scrutinizing Sid. In a way, he resembled Amulya Uncle, though sharper, far more intense. There was this sense of comfort with himself that showed through. It made him seem laid-back and at peace. Contradictory to how uppity and impatient he seemed, he'd been the nicest to me among everyone in the household. I hadn't realized it but that had mattered to me. More than I cared to admit. And my ears picked the strains of the lead guitar more prominently, tuning into the complexity and the beauty of its sounds.

During the next break, pizzas were ordered and the guys washed it down with gallons of beer. I only realized how late it was when I saw the deserted streets on the drive back. At my door I paused—still bemused, still overwhelmed.

'Thank you, Sid. It was a unique experience for me. I had a very nice evening.'

But halfway to his door, he neither stopped nor did he seem to hear me.

6

Riding on the Wind

A large household is replete with human drama even in the best of times. The vantage of a quiet observer is perhaps the most educational. For one, I was witness to the dynamics of married couples close up. While the elders seemed stable enough, their annoyances and skirmishes were direct, no holds barred, also, thankfully, humorous and brief. The interactions between Tony and Jayashree were far more theatrical—tensions drawn-out and reconciliations almost cloying.

Despite the united front they presented, the bloodcurdling six had their own share of falling out. At times, the sniping resumed at a meal with the rest of the family present. No one paid any attention to any of it, perhaps inured to it all through the years. Though there had been this rather unpleasant scene with Jayashree stomping upstairs to allege terrible ganging up against Tony, who had sat squirming through the entire tirade. Amulya Uncle and Aunty Shubhra had rushed to assuage her that the matter would be looked into. I am told Tony was made to pick the tab for everyone's beer that weekend. And there, thankfully the matter rested.

The visit to Sid's band I considered a one-off—just a stray gesture to try and assimilate me further into life here. Nothing had prepped me for when he caught up with me after I'd done the rounds with the incense sticks. I opened the cardboard box to find an unfamiliar radio-like gadget inside.

'So you can practise as you should.'

He stretched across my bed to find a plug point and switched it on. He turned a couple of knobs and the soothing strains of a tānpurā filled my room.

'It's an electronic tānpurā!' I had heard of them. 'Aren't these things terribly expensive?'

He was sitting on my bed now while I stood nearer the doorway, still uneasy. He seemed to be thinking of something.

'Why haven't I heard you practise any more?'

'I don't like to when I know there are others around.'

'Why? Are you self-conscious? Or is it that you don't want to disturb the others?'

I didn't know what to say. These were things I couldn't easily talk about. Conversation with him still seemed stilted.

'My music room is soundproof. Practise there, every day.'

'I thought I wasn't to step into your rooms.'

'You can. You even have permission to invade my rooms every evening with your foul incense, if you like.'

Despite the seeming levity, he looked at me with eyes that told me he was evaluating and hesitant. And what he said next came as a shock.

'How would you like to join our band, Disha? All the guys see potential in you and think you would enhance the music we play.'

'You are all rock musicians!'

'Yes, we mainly play bluesy rock. Yet, we constantly challenge boundaries trying to make our music more culturally relevant to our audiences. The aim is to build new synergies within our various musical influences—among which we count Hindustani classical and folk as well.'

'You know I am not good enough for performances.'

'Of course you are. All of us know that. We are a professional band. We wouldn't stake our reputation on someone we don't believe in. Let me be frank with you. It is not that there aren't people who are as good if not better. The issue is that we always find a reluctance to blend or to innovate. And to sing in a rock band, a classical musician is required to always battle the unfamiliar.'

'No, Sid. It's impossible!'

'So you want to sit and sing in darkened rooms hoping no one will hear you for the rest of your life?'

His words touched upon a deeply buried desire for performances that had flickered to life after the two unrehearsed pieces I had sung at the Pujo pandal. Until then, I had been unsure it could happen in a strange city. Not that it seemed possible even now.

'To me, music is deeply personal. I want to sing only for myself.'

'Then why do you have a voice? Why did you cultivate

it? You could just sing in your mind. Be reasonable, at least.'

'If I don't want to sing for you, it doesn't mean I am unreasonable.'

'You are not going to sing for me or for any other guy in the band. You are going to sing for yourself because you are a musician and all musicians need an audience who can appreciate what they do.'

'I can't do it. I'm sorry.'

In a rock band? Was he crazy?

He had expressive eyes and I saw him search my face closely as if he could read something no one else could.

'Don't shut doors. You owe yourself an honest effort.'

I was clutching at straws now. 'Did the others think I was good enough?'

'I don't know why their opinion matters more than mine. But yes, they did. It was unanimous.'

'I don't know rock music.'

'You aren't expected to as of now. But you will need to learn and practise a lot harder. A band is not about how good you are but how well you can synchronize and synergize with the musical prowess of all the others in your band.'

'Will you be there, Sid?'

'No, the plan was to quit the band the moment you joined.'

I liked that slow-spreading smile. His offer was momentous; it offered a path I had never imagined myself taking. Any person with half a brain cell would have leapt at the offer. And I was trying my best to dissuade him. Just that it was too big—so big that it was scary. I needed reassurance.

'Is it true what you said the other day? That you feel I am like a sister.'

A shutter fell in his eyes. Guardedness dropped as a steel cage around him, as it always did.

'I have two sisters. I have no place for another.'

'Why did you say it then?'

It hurt—this obvious snub.

'What did you want me to do? Tell the guys that I was violating our no-girls policy with a woman absolutely unrelated?'

'Then why did you take me along?'

He looked at me for a while, steadily.

'There are seven other young men floating about the house. Take your pick and find your brother among them.'

It is a symphony of black and light. All the equipment are black metal behemoths discernible from the shadows only through the mediation of thin films of hesitant light. Earlier on the sets than the technicians, I sit, trying to read and stay out of the way, as people walk around gingerly, prepping for the day ahead. These memories, like most, mortify me. How anxious was I for Sid's approval. How eager to find any form of kinship.

As it turns out, the brother surrogate came from someone who had been the most dreaded prankster—Joe. The cousin cartel too, I mused, had just needed a little getting used to.

They remained brash and unpredictable, yet I knew now their hearts were in the right places, and moreover, they were gentler on me. In the way that gradual familiarity weaves bonds between strangers, all of them grew into fraternal figures too. No day went by without seeing them, if only in passing, as time gradually enmeshed all our lives.

Sometimes, family dynamics fall into a groove of habit and fail to keep pace with newer realities. Tags remain. Everybody almost unconsciously continues to treat Joe half as a baby and half as the target of all their ribbing. No one notices that he holds his own among the motley crew at home, especially the two remarkable characters that are his older brothers. If there is an elephant in the room, only Joe will brave it, to articulate just what everyone wishes to avoid. There is a rare uprightness—a sort of moral fortitude that the family seems not to notice or give much credit to.

More than anybody, he speaks up for me in family discussions, even when I wish to simply acquiesce and have the focus shift from me. It is the most unlikely of alliances. Yet, in the family, Joe kind of adopted me.

༄

It took a lot of adjusting to, the idea that I'd be up there singing with the band. My mind oscillated fiercely between exhilaration and complete terror at failing and letting everyone down. I wished I could tell Sid it was all a mistake. That was the safe way. A tiny voice in my head reassured me that if I really tried, I could pull it off. That way, I could rescue my music from the silence it was fading into.

Now it sounded like a bolt from the blue at the table.

'Dad, did Disha tell you she has a job now?'

'What job?' I asked before anyone else could. Sid turned to me.

'You get paid per practice session. And you get paid even more per gig. I told you we were a pro band.'

He addressed his father and the others at the table.

'What band?' Aunty Karen seemed surprised, and not in a nice way.

'You know what band, Ma.'

'Yes, but what can she do in a rock band?'

'Our long search for a classically trained musician has ended. And now Disha is our new female vocalist.'

'Do you sing?' Aunty Parul and Aunty Shubhra questioned in a chorus.

I nodded, aware that everybody was staring. On their faces, too, I saw the doubt that paralysed my mind.

'Does that mean she will now keep the hours you do? That's not possible, you know!' Aunty Karen interjected.

'I will be there. Disha will be with me at all times. I can't see why not.'

The idea didn't seem to calm her.

'Your timings are all erratic. I think it will be impossible. No, I don't see how she can join your band.'

'It's not your call,' Sid challenged her and their eyes held, unwavering, antagonistic.

'Don't get all possessive of Sid now, Ma.'

Nina spoke so rarely that everyone stopped eating. Aunty seemed furious and had to strain to keep her tone even.

'I'm not being possessive of Sid. It's just that it's...it's not right. I don't see how someone should expect us to put up with those hours.'

'Lila did. All my brothers do. I do, sometimes. Ma, Sid likes Disha. A lot. Get used to the idea.'

There was pin-drop silence at the table. All the discreet ones looked down at their plates. I felt my mouth go dry. I didn't understand why Nina was saying what she was. The gang of six looked on agog, elated there was a skirmish in the offing.

'Nina, Sid has a list of girlfriends as long as your arm. We are all used to it, me especially. It goes with being a star. Please don't put ideas into her head. She comes from a remote village and lacks the exposure all of you have had. Now that Amulya has brought her here, I can only make sure she is fed, clothed and okay until we can marry her off. And joining a rock band is a step in the wrong direction. Sid should know that too.'

I noticed Amulya Uncle look at Sid for a long moment. Almost in confusion, he turned to me briefly before returning to him.

'Do you think Disha is right for you?'

'She is, Dad. We need her. And as a musician, she needs this too.'

'Your ma is not all wrong. Disha is not used to our ways. And though your band has always been stable, some do implode, you know. An addition could strain the already established synergies. Do you think you can take care of her despite?'

'She is an adult, for heaven's sake. She'll be just fine.'

'You do know she's not twenty-one yet? There is a reason I've brought her here to live with us.'

Sid looked thunderstruck. 'Are you just twenty?'

I nodded, miserable, hoping everyone would find something else to talk about.

7

Walking on the Moon

I hadn't noticed Amit had come to sit next to me when a technical snag held up the actual shooting and the ever-welcome cigarette break was called out. He sat in a peaceful silence so his question was in a way unanticipated. 'Why is it that every time we ask you a question about the past, you seem lost?'

I try to make light of it as I reply with a question of my own. 'Lost?'

'Each question nudges you into the haze of the past which you seem to wish to inhabit with greater happiness than your present.'

'It's not like that. Perhaps these are opportunities to revisit memories I may have somehow blocked.'

He took a deep drag of his cigarette, thinking for a while.

'It will all work out for you, Disha. I have a special understanding when it comes to these things.'

When I got back to the room from my bath, Sid was lying in my bed, his palms supporting his head on the pillow. He seemed completely at home there. I stopped at the door, watching him, a little apprehensive at the sense of reassurance his presence brought to the room.

'How long do you take a bath for? I've been waiting for hours.'

'And why have you been waiting?'

'I need to talk to you again. Part of an interminable series of talks I intend to bore you with.'

Standing beside the bed, I tried not to let this bundle of fears regarding joining the band disconcert me. The aura around Sid made me wary, especially now after Nina's comments.

'It's time to go down for breakfast.'

He looked at his watch. It had a thick steel rim and a square navy-blue dial.

'There are good twenty minutes to breakfast.'

He moved to make place for me on the bed. 'I need you to sit first and pay attention.'

As I did, he reached out and tugged at the towel I had turbaned around my sodden hair.

'Go put this in the laundry basket. And where are your other used clothes?'

The meaning of my silence he read and it seemed to irk him.

'You've washed them and put them out to dry on the terrace, haven't you? Damn! What is wrong with you?'

He bunched the towel and threw it across the room, almost angrily.

'If I had the slightest clue that you are so young I never would have taken you to meet the guys. Now that I have and you are supposed to join us, there's no backing out.'

'What does my age have to do with my ability to sing?'

'Your ability to sing is the crux, but there's more, particularly when it comes to being a part of a band and in the constant company of a group of oversensitive musicians. For that you need the maturity to make sure you do not crack from within.'

'What makes you think I lack maturity?'

He seemed to be in deep thought and held out his palm, almost distracted.

'Disha, give me your hand.'

I guess I wanted to prove my maturity. I held it out almost as a test. His eyes bore into me. 'And do you trust me?'

Warmth flooded me and words fled. I nodded.

'Being an artiste, any artiste, is a life of heartbreak. The only thing that makes it all worthwhile is your passion and that community which can understand the art and you. Tell me, Disha, reassure me that my desire to have you perform on stage to appreciative audiences instead of the solitude of dark rooms is not misplaced.'

'I am unsure I have the merit.'

'All of us are. But can you take the journey, whatever it demands?'

'I don't know what it demands.'

'What if it demands that you feel deep hurt and pain, betrayal and darkness? What if it demands that you feel joy and peace beyond what you have ever imagined before? Or it means no longer being safe and sheltered?'

'You are scaring me.'

'I am merely warning you. It will be tough.'

It felt nice to have Sid hold my hand and talk to me so earnestly. His voice was gentle. He held my palm tighter now. 'I give you my word that I will try my best to make the journey pleasant, even worthwhile. But I require you trust me—that I always know what you are feeling and thinking, that you let me know where you are at all times.'

He lay there, talking, while I relaxed in this unexpected intimacy until it was time to go down for breakfast. His mother noticed that we had come in together and she watched as Sid pulled out a chair for me to sit before he sat to my right. We were served coffee, and after a couple of sips, I asked Ronny to pass the milk jug so I could make the coffee milder.

'How is Monica these days, Sid? It has been ages since we've seen her. You must invite her to spend a day here,' Aunty's question seemed conversational.

'If Sid wants her over, he'll call her. Why do you need to invite his friends over?' his father wanted to know.

'Monica is fine. She is in Denmark on a project and will be there for another month, at least,' Sid informed his mother.

Aunty Karen began thinking out loud. 'I really like that girl. She has so much class and is a real beauty too.'

That fulsome praise seemed to miff Jayashree. 'I don't think she is *that* great. She comes off as hard and artificial, too career-minded and full of herself.'

In that strain of awkwardness, only Joe was grinning. 'Joy, you need not get jealous and catty. She is Sid's girlfriend, not Tony's.'

Jayashree bristled, 'I was just expressing my opinion. Ma seems to think too highly of her.'

'So this is the war of the daughters-in-law? Don't worry, our man Sid will just continue to have his string of girlfriends and a bevy of adoring babes and marry no one. Your real competition will be my wife. Only there'll be no competition at all as she'll be a perfect angel.'

'And which perfect angel will marry you?' Aunty Shubhra wanted to know.

'I can't tell you, Aunty. They keep falling over themselves trying to get to me,' Joe clarified.

'What happened to Rubina? We don't see her any more,' Aunty Parul was curious.

Joe sighed. 'Turns out she wasn't as angelic as I thought she was.'

'You can't keep having a new relationship every three months, Joe!' Aunty Shubhra admonished him.

'Why does no one lecture Sid for being a womanizer? And me, I don't want it that way. Seems I only attract the fly-by-night, sipping-and-flitting variety of girls.'

Aunty Karen hotly defended Sid. 'Sid is not a womanizer. It's just that a lot of women are interested in him. It's that rock star image.'

'Accept it. Sid is a total womanizer, Ma. It's just that you cannot see any fault in your gem of a special son.'

'I agree, Aunty Karen. Even after all these years, kids in our college still speak of Sid's magic over girls in awe,' Dave contributed.

'He never took to the stage there with less than five b... bits of feminine inner wear being flung at him,' Ronny added.

Amulya Uncle sounded weary. 'Can we have breakfast in peace, without being inappropriate?'

'You can do more. You can hold your head high as the proud father of a true-blue stud. Sid has a reputation!'

8
Peaceful Easy Feeling

Deena had invited me to spend a day with her. She would come over to pick me up sometime around mid-morning. Ashok, my brother-in-law, had kept the day free of any business obligations and the promise was that lunch would be at his favourite restaurant so I would be able to sample just what culinary treats Kolkata's finest had to offer. It felt wonderful. I would be seeing my sister after what felt like an era. Suddenly, I felt as if my world had widened a little. There was another place to go, another set of people who would have me, for however brief a duration.

It was deep in the afternoon when I received a hurried call from Deena on the family's telephone line, informing me the plans for lunch were cancelled and she would get back to me later. I swallowed my disappointment as I reassured her it was fine. Yet, that childlike feeling of being let down tinged with negative feelings persisted till evening. More importantly, it underlined the fact that everyone else's life and concerns excluded me. Perhaps that is how it is for all grown-ups. And in one way or another, I would have to create a world of my own.

The next meeting with the band was scheduled ten days away. I threw myself into riyāz with greater fervour. I had taken to using the tānpurā in Sid's music room as he sat by reading a book or fiddling with his laptop on a large lounger of a chair, though I knew his ear was on every note that I sang.

He reached to position another chair close beside his and picked up a guitar. 'What is your favourite rāg?'

'It varies.'

There was soft patience in the way in which he rephrased that. 'What is currently your favourite rāg?'

'It's Hamsadhvani. I've been told it isn't really a Hindustani classical rāg but borrowed from the Carnatic style. It's melodious.'

'Sing me the ārohan, avarohan and pakad.'

These were technical terms and I was surprised someone like him knew what they meant.

'How does a rock musician know these terms?'

'I just do. Now sing it.'

Always part of my repertoire, I sang the format effortlessly. When I was done, he strummed his guitar for a bit. Then he played a chord. 'This is your scale. You can sing an ālāp now.'

I hesitated. His tone was soft and carefully low. 'What now?'

'That guitar prompt sounds strange.'

Somehow, he managed to coax music out of my reluctance. As I sang, he followed as deftly as a harmonium player does. After a while, I stopped, almost mid-note.

'I understand you are trying to provide accompaniment, however, the alien sound is distracting.'

Wordlessly, he bent to his guitar and played little clusters of notes in which I could recognize scrambled syllables of a soulful Hamsadhvani. I marvelled anew at what a superb musician he was. Gradually, I joined him, making an effort to sing again. What he played in the background still waylaid me, though I was determined to hold my own and managed to sing along for a while. Finally, he put his guitar down.

'How far have you studied?'

'I'm a Science graduate, majored in Zoology.'

This close I couldn't see his face, just the dark depths of his eyes. Yet, somehow, I could never read what he was thinking.

'Suppose you get a job in an office now. You would not use even 5 per cent of the stuff you have studied. Do you know that?'

I knew. I nodded to convey that.

'What your graduation would have, ideally should have, taught you, are life skills—handling issues and people, using data, adaptability, management of time and resources, understanding your strengths and yourself better as well as the people around you.'

'I suppose so.'

'It's the same with your classical tāleem, the music education you have received. In an ideal world, you would have proceeded to complete your doctorate in Zoology or gone ahead to be a purist classical vocalist. But it isn't an ideal world, is it?'

Somehow I wished it was.

'What do you hear now?'

I listened. I looked at him enquiringly.

'I hear nothing, Sid.'

'There are two things you can ordinarily hear—silence and noise. Only a chosen few hear a third option. Music. And out of little bits of organized noise and other bits of silence, they weave music until everyone can hear it and feel it too.'

This sounded profound. My eyes sought his. There was honey-textured light in them. Later, I realized this light in his eyes always came on when he played or spoke about music.

'What you have been taught as strict unbreakable rules, the taboos in your system of music, may not apply to those outside of it. Are you willing to challenge all that you have learnt? Can you believe in a higher music that transcends all, takes you beyond the boundaries of what you know?'

He brushed my cheek with light fingertips. 'Don't look so worried. And tell me when my lectures begin to scare you.'

☙

Sid persisted in assimilating me into the role he visualized as a vocalist in his band. He insisted I practise singing sitting on a chair, standing up or even kneeling down.

'In the pressures of a performance, you will suddenly find that you can only sing if you sit cross-legged as during your practice sessions and that will kill it.'

He would play his guitar as I practised. Sometimes, his runs would go counter to mine, almost throwing me off, making it impossible to hold my own against him. But slowly—almost excruciatingly slow—I learnt to sing until I was on the verge of collapse from the intricacies of his notes. I adapted to artfully collapsing into him, singing his melody for a while before departing on my solo flight again.

Throughout, he would correct me gently, nudging me in the right direction through an alternate demo. And by insisting, I layer my sound on the established tracks he taught me to experiment and get to know the possibilities of my vocal range better. Increasingly complex tasks were set by mapping out in strict precision the number of beats and just how elaborate my contribution was to be, the expectation of the mood and feel, and then, I was given the free hand to innovate. I almost never disagreed with him or threw rules at him, knowing instinctively that his judgement in music was impeccable. We also spent a lot of time listening to concerts on his system. He would pause and rewind to point out the finer nuances or to tell me about the background of the pieces. In time, this became my whole world. When I would go back to sleep, the music stayed with me, playing even in my dreams.

One evening, I was yawning.

'I don't think I can go on tonight, Sid. I'm really sleepy now.'

Keeping the guitar aside, he stood up. And then, he bent to kiss me on my cheek. For a moment, I froze, unable to look up. Then I moved to the door, as casual as I could be. This was the first time any man had come this close, kissed me, however innocuously. I could still feel the heat where his lips had been, very briefly, against my cheek.

'His mother is British. This is just goodnight. It's normal.' I kept reminding myself. The entire household was very demonstrative, too. But it was a messy tangle of thoughts that kept me awake deep into the night.

❧

'There's a meeting at three, Sid. You should be done and out by five, latest,' his youngest uncle Atulya informed him at breakfast.

'Yeah, I know. I'd seen the mail. But I hadn't been sent a copy of the agenda. Anything I need to know beforehand?'

'I expect the usual. It's a routine meeting.'

Aunty Karen turned to me with a tight smile. 'I'll hold you responsible in future if Sid neglects his duties at the office like this.'

I looked down at my plate, uncomfortable, not sure what I needed to say.

'Disha isn't Sid's wife. Yet. Why should she be responsible for him or his actions?' Joe challenged his mother.

His words annoyed her intensely, but she tried to answer with a gracious smile. 'Sid is completely absorbed in his idea of a female vocalist for the band. He is not quite aware that it's just that—an idea.'

'Isn't that Sid's business?'

'Well, if she is good enough to be in the band, she shouldn't need all this training and hand-holding or whatever. Sid has obligations and duties. In fact, Sid has enough to do without more burden.'

Sid seemed to have not heard a word. He was looking at me with a twinkle. 'So how come you aren't frowning at your coffee this morning? Actually, what you drink is not coffee at all. It's pure milk needing the coffee only to disguise itself.'

9

Another One Bites the Dust

Though I had not gotten over my dread of young men in groups and probably never would, I had learnt to acclimatize to them and their ways. And that helped immensely when I needed to integrate with the band, spending large chunks of my days in their company.

Of the lot, Vidyut is the darling. He seems to be the only one who recognizes I am a woman and that I am new to their setup. He will insist that I take breaks, and talks to me about a host of things, just to draw me further into their group. At mealtimes, he serves me food and keeps an eye out on how much I eat while the rest of the band just grabs what they can in large quantities.

Ashraf is shy—the deep one. He only speaks about music and usually only to Shady and Sid. Shady, on the other hand, is voluble and indiscreet. He often has to be asked to shut up. Nishith mostly keeps to himself. There is something edgy and disenchanted about him. He brings strange new music on his iPod to each practice session and revels in introducing new sounds to the others. All that quietens when he sings. Every sound he utters has a mesmerizing tonality.

In time, it was apparent that Sid leads the band. Very subtly, without being demanding or autocratic, he schedules the practice sessions and he chooses the kind of music they play. His knowledge and understanding of music is phenomenal, and the others respect this and his natural leadership. There is a practical and almost mundane, administrative side to running a band as well. There are accounts, finances, and other decisions to be made. It isn't simple work and all the others rely on Sid's experience and expertise from his alternate career in his dad's firm.

The early days of intense coaching that Sid had made me undergo stood me in good stead, and though musically the band seemed all unfamiliar and daunting still, I began to relate to it. I have been told the band has a 'no-girls and no-covers' policy, though their repertoire does contain about five rock anthems creatively reengineered to sound nothing like the originals. Their music is bilingual, the lyrics of their songs in both English and Bangla.

At break, Sid was by himself, his fingers flying over the strings of his guitar—a frown of concentration keeping him removed from small talk. I took a cup of tea for him. He put the instrument down to take it and when he looked up, it seemed he wanted to say something. I paused.

Something was clouding his face. Yet he said nothing, and after maybe a minute or two, he got up to join the guys.

My first song was to be the same bhātiyāli I had sung

to them the first time. I had half-expected Sid to rev up the tempo to make it rock and relevant. But he retained the original scheme, overlaying it with beautiful sounds of the keyboard and guitar. I was amazed to hear our first recording of the finished song. All of us heard it being played as we snacked and sipped tea.

'Nishith, how would it be if you didn't come in for the chorus? Let's reverse things and have you both sing the verses together and have Disha sing the chorus alone,' Sid suggested. 'And, Disha, you have to come up with a longer ālāp and further elaborations before you launch into the chorus each round.'

After dinner, we tried out his suggestions until everyone was satisfied with how it sounded.

'That will be your song for your debut appearance,' Sid consulted the tiny calendar on his phone. 'Nine days from now, next Saturday.'

'Stage appearance? This soon?'

The others fell silent. Sid was unperturbed. 'You've heard the recordings. You are ready to go on stage nine minutes from now.'

There were two other songs I was to participate in. One was an up-tempo Bangla original. Nishith and I were to engage in a sawāl-jawāb segment with him singing fragments of the song and me responding with notes within the framework of similar beats. For the English number there was a very slow beginning that demanded almost crooning, with Nishith and me taking turns. When Nishith was done, I was to provide a large space of soothing background notes before Sid took off in a long intricate riff, turning the sound into a darker, heavier metallic rock until Vidyut found the beat, going demonic on the drums. The sudden metamorphosis worked, which made me happy. More importantly, I understood my part in each composition and how I synchronized with the band.

It was past eleven and pack-up had been declared. I sat on the floor watching the others unplug their instruments and cover them for the night. Vidyut came to sit beside me, a friendly arm around my shoulders, asking whether I was tired.

I turned to smile at him. 'A little. You?'

'Sid and I have been at this for twelve years now. We began in Class X, when we were both fifteen. Either of us can go on all night.'

So Sid was twenty-seven. I knew the twins, Ronny and Danny, were touching thirty and were ribbed about their advancing years a great deal, but somehow Sid had seemed older, somehow more responsible. I looked around the room for him. Our eyes met for a moment. I saw the look which made me feel like he wanted to say something return in his eyes, but then he went back to dismantling his guitar and amp.

'Disha, what do your parents say about you being in a band? Don't they want to meet all of us sometime?'

'My parents are dead. I thought you knew, all of you. Sid's dad is now my guardian. These days, I live in their house.'

Something prompted Vidyut to remove his arm from around me. He looked thoughtful for a bit.

'Are you and Sid close?'

'Not really. Apart from the music, we have nothing else in common.'

Both of us looked at Sid now. He went towards the door and then turned, his fingers on the handle. I got up quietly.

'Be seeing you, Vidyut.'

Nishith watched me as I walked past him, his eyes dark and intense. He blew me a kiss. 'Take care, Disha.'

'Good night, Nishith. Good night, guys.'

'Aren't you taking your guitar tonight?' I asked Sid in the car.

He didn't answer but concentrated on his driving, speeding recklessly along the abandoned streets. I leaned forward and switched on the CD system and music filled the car. The lead vocals were awesome, stamped with an unmistakable timbre, throbbing raw electric power. I was about to turn to Sid for help in identifying the band and the voice when he switched it off abruptly.

'I've had enough noise for one evening, thank you.'

'I thought it was all music. And you are a musician.'

'Why are you arguing with me?'

'I am not arguing. I was just...'

Hurt, I turned away to concentrate on the desolate shuttered shops that lined the roads. Instead of parking in the huge garage sheds at the side of the house, Sid stopped outside the gates to drop me off.

'Aren't you coming home?'

He refused to answer.

'Are you upset with me, Sid? Have I said or done

something?'

I waited for his reply while he made it clear he was just waiting for me to get off before he could drive away. A cold clammy constriction took over my chest. I realized I had not told Vidyut how it was. I felt close to no one as I did with Sid. And for all the time and effort he seemed to spend on me, he still remained a distant continent—unknown and forbidding.

Ranjan Uncle let me in.

'Have you eaten dinner?'

'Yes, have you?'

'I was just about to go to bed myself. Now Suresh will attend to all else that needs to be done.'

Everyone was either asleep or still out. I encountered no one on the way. The feeling that something was amiss persisted, and after changing into my nightclothes, I lay in bed, trying to read. This was the first time the tiny white phone by my bedside had rung. I answered with a tentative 'hello?' more to cut that shrill discordant ringing in a now somnolent household.

'Did I wake you up?' There was silence for a bit. 'Were you sleeping?'

'No, I was reading.'

'Go to sleep. You should take extra good care of your throat with the performance just over a week away.'

'Is that what you've called to say?'

He hesitated. I got the feeling that a lot mattered in each word he spoke, yet nothing made sense.

'Where are you, Sid?'
'Why?'
'I just wanted to know.'
'I'm out.'

This pause was long and awkward. I broke it. 'Good night, then.'

He didn't respond. I just heard the click of the call being disconnected.

10

Blinded by the Light

If I had thought that was the lowest trough in my interactions with Sid, I was much mistaken. There had always been unease. In him, I sensed mild impatience, which made me wonder why he bothered to engage with me at all. It was either that or retreating behind a wall of silence. It didn't feel good to be frozen out. On my part, there was a determined tilt to my chin not to be overawed by his celebrity status. And there was genuine perplexity in figuring out what made him this unpredictable. The mix was volatile.

Sid was taking me to find a costume for my stage appearance. I only wore salwar-kameez or sarees on formal occasions and would be horribly self-conscious in anything else. But I didn't want to verbalize my fears. The band was aware that the standard jeans, faded T-shirt and a vest could not apply to me. Female artistes project an image and Nishith voiced the concern that my image ought to gel with the band's.

'We just make damn good music, that's all we need to

project. Disha is a brilliant singer, and she could be in rags or in an evening gown, nothing will change that fact,' Vidyut refuted hotly.

Shady had understood Nishith's point of view. 'No, guru, the image matters. There'll be at least 60 per cent dick-heads in the crowd who don't understand the music anyway.'

'So we don't cater to them.' This had been Ashraf.

'Leave Disha's costume to me. The two of us will go and pick out something suitable,' Sid had ended the discussion.

As the concert neared, the butterflies in my tummy went berserk in stages. Tony brought it up at breakfast.

'I saw the posters for the Rock for All Concert on Friday. Derozio Dreams is the star attraction.'

'Yeah, we're on this Saturday.'

Danny was curious. 'Is Disha there too?'

'It's her debut. Don't miss it.'

'I demand we be given guest passes.'

'It's a sponsored ticketless concert, Joe. What do you need passes for?'

'If my beloved big bro is in the band, I'd better be hobnobbing with VIPs.'

All the guys thought the same and there were chaotic demands for passes for a while.

'I'll organize five passes. Ma, Dad, Nina, Tony and Jayashree will get them. That's all.'

'What have your uncles done to you?' Achintya Uncle demanded to know. 'Your dad is a Rabindra Sangeet purist. All the rock you ever heard in this house, you heard from me.'

'Not true. I sent him for piano lessons when he was just four,' Aunty Karen objected, laughing.

'That almost put him off music for life.'

'The organizers don't bargain for twenty plus family members. I'll get the five passes and you can have your free-for-all without involving me.'

'I don't like your kind of music,' Jayashree informed Sid.

'Great. Uncle, there is your pass.'

'You're wrong, Joy. Sid's band is incredible. You should hear them in concert once,' Tony tried to coax her.

'If a nobody from Hamirpur can so easily become a member of the band, how good can it be?' was Jayashree's argument. No one responded and she continued cattily, 'Anyway, if you flop miserably, Disha, you have an alternative career. That fish you made the other day was passable. You can always find a little something to do in a restaurant or join as a staff in some catering business. Anything to save you from this life of being at the wrong end of handouts.'

'I'm glad you liked the fish, Jayashree. When you hadn't mentioned it, I was afraid it wasn't good enough.'

'You could cook some more, help around a little and be useful to the family sometime as you used to in the past. You can't always just hang out with the celebrity in the family and refuse to contribute. Everyone knows Dad is extremely generous and tolerant, but you shouldn't take advantage of his charitable nature.'

The guys started something down the table and though everyone heard and understood the full implication of what

Jayashree was saying to me, it was easy to pretend we were all too distracted to.

⁂

'Why don't you stand up to Jayashree? No one else can do that for you, you know.' Sid broke the silence in the car.

'I don't want to argue with her.'

We drove on some more. I don't know what prompted me to say what I did next. 'But Jayashree is only being forthright about what is on everybody's mind anyway.'

Sid shot me a glance. 'What do you mean?'

'I am practically a penniless orphan. I live off the bounty your father and your family provide me. Due to my father's acquaintance with your dad, I am a little above the servants. But I am clearly not equivalent to any family member.'

His voice was calm. I had no clue he was furious. 'And why do you feel this way?'

'I feel it very strongly.'

'Has anyone said anything suggesting this to you?'

'They don't need to. I understand the vibes.'

'I'm sorry, Disha. I had no clue you had so much garbage in your head. I'm certain, absolutely certain, not a single family member, including Jayashree, feels this way. If she is rude, she is rude to everybody, even to me.'

'What do you know, Sid? You haven't been at the receiving end.'

His voice was icy. 'So tell me, inform me.'

I went on heedlessly, without stopping to think. 'Aunty

Karen was most kind and accepting of me. But the day you first brought me to the band, it changed.'

'Why do you think that is?'

'As long as I knew my place and stayed out of all your lives, I was welcome. The moment I began interacting with her precious son a little more, like I am a person too, she just can't handle it.'

'I hope you realize you are talking about my mother. And Ma is the most important person in the world to me.'

I became silent, regretting that I had verbalized my thoughts.

'Is there a reason you can think of that I should sit here and listen to this tripe, this character assassination?'

'I'm sorry, Sid. But that's the truth.'

He was white with anger now. 'And I need a stupid, insensitive, ungrateful, poisonous twenty-year-old witch to tell me the truth!'

He made a rash U-turn; squealing tires, honking cars behind, glares from fellow drivers and all.

'I'm sorry. I can't take you shopping. In fact from this moment on, I refuse to have anything further to do with you.'

I could see his jawbone rigid as he drove recklessly through the early evening traffic, speeding homeward to get rid of me. We were forced to slow down to a crawl at a traffic light.

'Ma was trying to protect you.'

I had turned to stone and almost didn't hear him.

'You have heard all of them talk about it, about my

reputation with girls. I know a lot of them somehow. Not that there is a single among them that I would want to have anything to do with,' he paused to marshal his thoughts. 'My family thinks I am a commitment-phobic womanizer. I guess Ma is concerned I would play with you too and it would all end up in a sorry mess.'

I mulled this over in silence. 'Even Nina thought Aunty Karen was being possessive about you.'

He exploded now. 'Damn Nina! And damn you! I'm done talking sense to you. And just so that you know, you aren't that great, you miserable little rat, that my mother needs to feel insecure about you!'

I hoped to encounter no one on my way to my room. But just when I thought I was safe, I ran into Aunty Parul on the second-floor landing.

'Disha! What is wrong?'

I shook my head.

'Have you had a fight with anyone? Did any of the boys say something to you?'

'I just feel a little nauseous, that's all.'

And I rushed towards the shelter of my room. I had never felt this miserable before. I really did feel like throwing up. I spent all the time until dinner just hiding away in my room. Going down to dinner was a big effort. I made it because I knew I couldn't miss a meal unless I was at practice and had informed everybody well in advance. I still didn't have that much ease in the household. It was much later, when I just couldn't go to sleep, that it struck me. If the phone stored numbers in its memory, it would have Sid's number as the only call received recently.

Sid sounded furious still. 'Where the hell did you get my number?'

The words came in a stammer. 'You...you had called once.'

'Erase the damn number and never call me again.'

I tried to hold back my tears with a sniff. He didn't speak but he didn't disconnect either.

'No one else talks to me. Who will, Sid, if you won't?'

My words were met by a freezing silence.

'I thought I could be myself with you. I thought you were my friend. I thought you sincerely wanted to know what I was feeling and thinking.'

'I was wrong. I'm sorry if you were misled. Now please just leave me alone.'

11

A Whiter Shade of Pale

The next time I saw Sid was on the afternoon of the concert. He had been conspicuous in his absence at all meals so far. Thankfully, no one had remarked on it or wondered aloud where he was. I knew Aunty Karen scrutinized me every time she saw me, but I had learnt my lesson—dissociating from even perceiving or registering what she did.

I missed Sid terribly. His absence and the reasons for it had led to some of my bitterest, most miserable thoughts. My thirsting eyes stole a look at Sid. He seemed absolutely normal, unchanged in any way, though he seemed even quieter, more preoccupied during the meal. When everyone was winding up, he turned to his mother.

'I have fifteen guest passes for the family tonight. I'll leave them with you for all those who want to come.'

Then he addressed me without looking in my direction. 'The soundcheck is at four. We should leave home around three, Disha.'

'Do you want me there, Sid?'

'You know our music is loud and there'll be crowds. But there is a separate enclosure for guests, Ma. The concert begins at seven. There will be two acts, each hour-long, before us. So you can come later, maybe after an early dinner, around nine or so.'

I wanted to ask the same question again, but I was a little uncertain. I had thought that since that horrible spat, I wasn't going to be on stage any more. I didn't want to now. But I didn't dare say it as I wanted to avoid confrontations even more. We drove to the venue in near-perfect silence. I hoped Sid would say something—anything. But he lapsed into his old habit of pretending I wasn't there at all.

The concert was under the aegis of Rock for All, a series of performances that were free to the spectator, the costs being borne by a consortium of sponsors. I was told that normally three such concerts were held each year in Kolkata. It helped that the chief of this operation was a huge Derozio Dreams fan and the band was usually invited to perform at most of these events.

The moments before my nascent performance in a rock band seemed to warp, where various irreconcilable little events and experiences played out all too slow, like slivers of a broken mirror that reflected reality in discrete parts. And the background sounds only exaggerated their effect on my perceptions.

This evening's venue was an old government Science college—humungous grounds on either side of the sleepy inner road. While the smaller one was being used as a car park, the larger one was where the concert was to be held. Bands were permitted to drive up close to the stage to unload and only these vehicles were then taken to the tiny private parking in front of the college buildings. Vidyut and Shady were waiting for us and they helped Sid with all the stuff.

Sid pointed, 'That green bag is your kit, Disha.'

I leaned in to retrieve it and then stayed out of the way. Another band was undergoing their soundcheck. Their lead was off stage in front.

Screech shhshh shhhhhh Shrek check-cheque-czech...

'Heyyyy, Sid. Man!'

Happy embraces all around. Much warmth.

'Uttiyo, great to see you, dude. All set?'

'Yeah, almost. Stay with me. Tell me what you think.'

'Give me just a moment to go dump this.'

'Sure. Hey, I've got some great Manipuri stuff. A cousin brought it down specially and it's guaranteed to blow your mind.'

When it was time for our soundcheck, Vidyut began the proceedings, being extremely finicky. Sid went way behind and stood there communicating in gestures. Vidyut was communicating freely on the mike Ashraf held to him.

Boom crash bang... Poised drumsticks that went fuzzy in a beat.

'Give me more bass. It feels like I'm playing a blooming garbage can, dude.'

The sound engineer told him something on the feedback monitor that only those on the stage could hear.

'Why should more bass cause vibrations? You aren't tinkering with your grandma's stereo, you fucking nut! Pete, are you there?'

He seemed to have heard from Pete.

'Spare me this crap, boss. Do your job. What vibration is that wet-eared sob giving me grief over?'

And so it went.

Ashraf checked his keyboard by playing a Western classical piece that sounded so sublime that everyone around stood and clapped when he was done. Shady smoked a series of cigarettes and seemed casual as he slapped his palm along his guitar strings in near-drumming motions; he lingered until his sound was just perfect. Sid was monitoring it all from way beyond. He was to approach the stage next and he stopped by the sound console to confer. His soundcheck was the briefest, but the few bars he played sounded clear and throbbed with a wild energy. And whoever was in that space stopped what they were doing to listen to this hymn-like music

The surprise package was Nishith, who chose to sing extremely bawdy couplets in a hideous dialect that was way removed from the anglicized diction of his normal Bangla. His eyes held a strange gleam as he handed the mike to me with exaggerated care.

'Madam, all yours. The mike. And me.'

'No, where is Disha's mike?'

The sound guy on stage heard Sid and retrieved it from near the drum kit, switched it on and handed it to me. I stared at it, frozen. And then, I began to sing the Bāgeshri ālāp once more, missing Baba, missing my life as I had known it until recently, and now, missing Sid. Somehow, he'd stepped closer to the stage and now held up a hand for me to stop and turned to speak to the sound engineers there.

Even without a mike, the woman's shriek was clear in the faint evening breeze. Sid looked around with a smile. She was accompanied by a security guy in a luminescent orange vest who'd probably come along to verify whether she indeed knew the band. The force with which she flung herself into Sid's arms and how her fingers touched his face and hair and the kiss that followed left nobody in any doubt.

I waited for Sid's signal to resume. Vidyut prompted me. 'Go on, Disha. Sid is otherwise occupied. And as the evening progresses, it will only get worse.'

I now sang the drut composition in Bāgeshri which none of the guys had heard. The words in khari boli were about mourning a lost beloved. And for the first time I fully understood the loss the lyrics spoke of. Amongst the sparse audience, Sid had straightened and stood listening intently, though the babe still clung to him and looked ahead at me grudgingly. Sid left her behind as he walked up to me.

'Disha, hold the mike about an inch and a half closer. Let's see how that sounds.'

He went back to the stand next to the console. I began to sing the antarā part and he raised a thumb to tell me I sounded fine. Then the entire band took their places and we sang the Bangla number as a test piece.

With the prelim soundcheck done, the band had nothing much to do but slouch around in a dingy anteroom and talk meaninglessly—kind of a pre-performance holiday. Sid stayed back with the woman.

'I'll watch the show,' Ashraf declared.

'I'll come with you.'

And Shady and he set off.

With headphones on, Nishith sat slumped on the floor. Only Vidyut came to join me where I sat on a grimy tent-house chair. In time, it got completely dark. And the concert began outside. Some of the interrupted music floated by but only indistinctly. However, the roars of the crowd were unmistakable. When Sid returned to the room, the woman came with him. I noticed her body close against his. He rummaged through a bag and found something small that he put in his pocket.

'Annette, have you met Disha, our new vocalist?'

She looked at me, her expression bored.

'Yeah, I heard her sing.'

'Don't you want to rejoin the concert?'

She turned and moved even closer to him. 'No, sweets, I just want to spend some time with you.'

'And you know Vidyut and Nishith.'

Annette said some forced hi-s. Nishith looked at them wordlessly with curious eyes, interrupted when a flock of young women rushed into the room. Nina was among them and hung back as the others mobbed Sid, all pushing Annette out of the way. Everyone there seemed animated and Sid looked happier now than I had ever seen him, smiling as he teased and joked and posed for the phone cameras, genuinely content. It was a while before all of them decided to return to the concert, hugging and kissing him luck. Only Nina remained.

'Do you have a minute, Sid?'

'What is it, Nin? Excuse me, Annette.'

She waited around for a bit until it was evident that Sid wasn't going to be back anytime soon and left too. Someone had come by to leave a heap of bento boxes of Chinese food. I realized I was ravenous by now. Both Nishith and Vidyut used chopsticks impeccably and competed in picking up succulent pieces of chicken and prawns from my plate only to open more boxes and serve me copious amounts I couldn't eat. Competitive chop-sticking.

Sid came back a lot later, now purposeful. 'Time, guys. We ought to get ready.'

I hoisted the green bag I'd been given onto the counter in the large bathroom adjoining the hall. It held a couple of sealed bottles of water, four large bars of chocolate, a roll of wet wipes, a raspberry-flavoured lip gloss and a hairbrush. I tentatively reached out to touch the stuff, which he simply need not have bothered with. But there was something dutiful and dependable about Sid that I had come to admire. I recalled all the time he had spent so patiently mentoring me in the music room. Something very warm and beautiful had grown then. I had come to lean on him, to need him, far more than I should have. It felt like bitter regret that I had completely alienated him now.

The large packet at the bottom of the bag held a salwar in a jersey material styled to gather at the ankles and pleated down the front like a new-age harem pants. It went with a simple long coffee-coloured T-shirt with puff sleeves and narrow lace and ribbon trimmings. And instead of an odhna, there was a scarf in beige with olive green leaves. When I re-entered the room, all the guys stopped to stare. All except Ashraf, who had taken off his T-shirt and was hastily pulling the fresh one over his head now. Vidyut slowly came to where I stood.

'You look stunning, Disha. Even more beautiful than you normally do.'

And he bent to kiss the top of my head gallantly. I smiled up at him, but instinctively, my eyes sought Sid's approval. He had turned away.

⁂

There was frenzy amongst the crowd when the band was announced, with a sustained cheer and unending whistles. When Vidyut struck his drums, it dissipated into absolute stillness. One by one, other sounds joined him. And finally, Sid came on, his guitar wailing, sketching out fragments of promise that remained unfulfilled, unfinished.

I hadn't noticed Nishith next to me. He turned to me, and in that strange mix of light and dark, I could see the smile he shot me that was almost a leer.

'Oooohhhhh, she's fine!' he said it into the mike. The

crowd went ballistic. Sid turned to watch him. And then, Nishith sank to his knees as the spotlight found him and let out a crazy scream.

Our concert had begun.

12

Stairway to Heaven

*S*ome mornings, the chaos at the shoot is much controlled. Some mornings, the glitches and goof-ups are minimized and a sense of efficiency reigns, permitting all of us to go into our roles with ease. During one such briefing on a muggy Thursday morning, Param turns to give me the heads-up.

'So, Disha, today Juhi's question to you will be to briefly recall your experiences and memories of your first gig with Dreams. Perhaps you could write out the points and then see what you can pack in a couple of minutes of conversational dialogue.'

※

After the applause died down from a long instrumental piece mainly led by Sid and enriched with textures and weaves of surreal sound by both Ashraf and Shady, Nishith took up the mike again.

'Are you guys having fun?'

There was a thunderous applause.

He feigned deafness. 'I can't hear you.'

The noise shook the stage. 'Would you like to have twice the fun?'

The feedback from the audience almost deafened us. Nishith's voice went softer, taking on a seasoned RJ kind of tonality. 'This is a very special evening for Derozio Dreams. It is a new chapter in our history and one I hope will bring you even more joy from our music. Friends, please join me in welcoming our newest member—the lovely, the stupendous, Disha!'

Sid touched my shoulder lightly. 'Go, Disha.'

I stared at him, forgetting that there were thousands of witnesses, forgetting the magnitude of what I was about to embark upon. Just that Sid had spoken to me now was enough! I had to speak to him. I burned with the need to. But his urgent whisper reminded me where I was. I had lost myself in the molten warm light of Sid's eyes for that moment. And then, I recalled—it was all about the music.

Would the audience know that my soul lay in the strains of the introductory bars of my song? After I sang the first two phrases of notes, the crowd's reaction drowned my voice. I waited. Then, I repeated a minor variation. Nishith came to me and held me close, his arm scrunching my waist as we began the opening verse.

He let me go as I stepped forward, towards the blinding lights, and stood unseeing. My knees were almost wobbling now, even as I held my voice rock-steady and sang the chorus solo, imploring the boatman who held the key to my drift down the river to return to me.

When I paused, Sid and Ashraf took turns to draw out the melody to reaches our vocals could not venture at. And then, Nishith and I began the second verse again, standing a couple of feet apart, singing to each other. The appreciation from the crowd came as a tornado of applause.

'I guess you guys only have a lukewarm welcome for Disha,' Nishith joked.

The crowd refuted him.

'Give the lady some appreciation. Let her know you love her.'

The audience responded now, hysterical and loud.

'Over to you, Disha.'

I refused to speak as Nishith knew I would. Instead, I slipped into the faint background notes for the English number he was going to sing next. There were two encore performances at the end. Sid decided, for one, I should sing part of my piece again. And then, we had to stop for the night despite the requests for more. There was a deadline.

A bunch of roadies helped swiftly unplug the equipment under instructions from Sid and Vidyut. In the wings, Nishith held me to himself; his arms strong around me, holding me close against him, almost too tight. He was completely soaked in sweat and his body was still throbbing with the adrenaline from a successful performance. I stayed limp in his embrace.

'My darling Disha, you did wonderful!'

The crowds refused to leave and the security had to escort us back to the hall. Covering his eyes, Nishith collapsed on the floor—spent. Ashraf sat quietly, while Shady played a game on his phone. After a long wait, people were permitted to come into the hall on passing through a strict ID. We met Vidyut's parents. We knew them from all our practice sessions at their place.

'You were very good, Disha,' she was all smiles and encouragement. 'You held your own against these boys and they have all been pros for long now.'

Members of other bands came in too. And a whole lot of people I didn't know who didn't let small things like introductions get in the way of speaking animatedly to me. Then the unruly gang of six arrived, along with Tony. They mobbed Sid for a bit, excited, noisy, being physical and boyish, talking to him all at once while he bantered and tried to counter them. In that melee, Joe found me and put a concerned arm around me.

'Then why do you look so sad? Delayed stage fright?'

'Something like that.'

But my eyes wandered to where Sid seemed to be happy, soaking all the attention he was getting from the surge of people now. This was a Sid I didn't know—an animated voluble open extrovert who came alive in the company of people.

Joe's voice dropped. 'Don't let Sid or his antics upset you. The key is this, Disha, if he ever lets somebody into his life, he really cares for them.'

Others from the family came up to the two of us. Their dad was most appreciative. 'If I had known you were so good, I would have brought you here a couple of years ago and left you under Sid's wing. Makes me proud to have two musicians in the family!'

Aunty Karen didn't say anything. Only later did she turn to me. 'We are leaving now. You must be tired. Come home, it's quite late already.'

I didn't know Sid had heard it. 'The band needs to meet for a while after this, there's stuff to do.'

'Stuff? You will just drink and party. Why does she need to be there?'

'Disha can't go. She's part of the band. I'll bring her in a bit later.'

'Let her be, Karen. She deserves her bit of fun too,' Amulya Uncle reasoned. 'It's her debut night. It's a big night for her. And she's with Sid.'

Her expression was eloquent, but I turned away, refusing to read any of it.

I was taken to be introduced to Tapan Ghose, the moving spirit behind this series of concerts. He was smiling and reticent, though he wished me graciously on my debut. His fondness for Sid was apparent as the two of them stood together at the edge of the crowd, conversing solemnly.

Vidyut brought around his large minivan and all the equipment was loaded in it. Willing hands helped. Annette found Sid again in this melee. His hands dug into his pockets.

'I'm sorry, Annette. I am going to be really busy now. I won't tell you I'll call you tomorrow, I'll probably be exhausted. Sometime next week. Take care.'

She looked crestfallen but mustered a smile. 'I'll wait for your call, Sid.'

But he had already turned away to help Ashraf with his keyboard.

༄

We regrouped at our practice hall at Vidyut's place. I wasn't permitted to help or carry anything and instead tried to take care of lighter stuff like the masses of wires and cords, and to stay out of everyone's way.

There was a strange kind of energy that was unleashed now. I think it was partly relief, partly the high from a great performance and partly the fact that there were little boys even in macho rock musicians. For some unfathomable reason all of them wanted to give Shady bumps, and he resisted, running harum-scarum around the hall, knocking into things, until Sid tackled him and he was lifted off his feet. Despite all his resistance, he was kicked really hard on his butt numerous times.

Sid found a packet of some brown mass and handed it over to Vidyut. 'Uttiyo gave me this stuff. It smells really potent.'

Nishith had unearthed an unseemly quantity of bottles and he took deep swigs out of a squat one. And I was introduced to the flip side of being part of a rock band. The guys drank a lot of really smelly alcohol, almost neat. And those high spirits only got more raucous and unbridled. By now, Vidyut had prepared the mass, crumbling the leaves expertly and rolling joints for everyone. No one seemed to notice I was there too. Sid had almost finished smoking his second joint when he did.

'I'm sorry, guys. The lady and I have to go.'

'Stay back tonight and party. All of us are.'

'Can't. I should be taking Disha back.'

'Then you should have let her go with your mom.'

Sid didn't respond. He looked at the tip of his joint and then extinguished it against the neck of an empty bottle and left it on the table.

The drive back was as silent as all the others. And as usual, I tried to orient myself to the route we were taking by trying to identify the few landmarks I had learnt to recognize. Somehow the unspoken seemed to fog the air. But it seemed that only I was battling it.

'Is there water in here? I'm thirsty.'

I reached for the bag Sid had given me and unsealed a bottle to hand to him.

'Didn't you drink any?'

I shook my head. He had slowed down to drink. Now he looked at me, searching. His voice had dropped. 'I had warned you, the journey is tough.'

I sat inert, disengaged.

'Hadn't I?'

I turned my face to the window, hoping I could control the inexplicable tears that threatened. He took the car off the main road into the side of a deserted arterial road and stopped. I felt a couple of fingers stroke my hair.

'Twenty years old, Disha, you did far better than I dreamed.'

His voice sounded hurt at my silence.

'Why won't you talk to me? Haven't people lost their cool with you before?'

He waited for me to speak. I think he sensed that I was crying.

'Okay, don't talk. You don't need to do a single thing you don't want to.'

His hands somehow persuaded me to turn as he leaned towards me and held me to himself stiffly, almost as if he was duty-bound to.

'Just be where I can see you. Just be with me sometimes. Be happy.'

I stayed in his embrace with the same limpness I had in Nishith's. Except, Sid's proximity didn't feel the same. His palms stroking my back created warmth, a sense of homecoming I had not experienced before. I felt his cheek rest against the side of my head.

The tears wouldn't stop now and I cried freely—not knowing what I mourned, not knowing how deep the pain in me lurked. He held me a little puzzled perhaps in a way retreating, reverting to his familiar role of a guide and mentor.

'I am just glad we have got our first disagreement out of the way, Disha. We can now be level with each other, like two adults.'

I looked up at him, my tears stopping, distracted by

what I saw. This was Sid, in whose company each experience remained indelible in my memory. This was Sid, who never raised his voice or gave up, whatever levels of exasperation I may have caused him all through my music training. This was Sid, the only person I now knew, everybody else just acquaintances, to whom my existence meant really nothing.

And in his face, I saw something I never had before. This wasn't the aloof Sid everyone held in such awe. He was confused and pliable, very vulnerable somehow, and he seemed to be asking me for my understanding as well. And I comprehended that even though it was momentary each of us needed this microcosm of complete validity, the comfort that grew in that constricted space just then and the need for that touch to sustain us as we dealt with who we were and what we desired.

His palms wiped my cheeks and he dried them against the plain black T-shirt he had worn on stage. I realized with a pang how exhausted he must be—he didn't need to deal with my meltdown just now. I tried to tell him that but he held a finger against my lips. We still couldn't look away from each other and a sort of hypnotic force built up that seemed to impel him to hesitantly bend down to my lips.

It surprised me that, for a while at least, I seemed to lead. It was my hand that reached for his face, the tip of my thumb feeling each bristle against his skin. His lips had just rested there but mine opened, telling him without words how I felt, how much he mattered—all that I could never begin to express in the cold light of sanity.

Our eyes shut as we moved closer, holding each other with needy fingers. Something inside us—primal, visceral, raging—was now communicating at levels neither of us knew or understood but reciprocated almost completely. And beyond all, its fury brought immense fulfilment and peace. I came back to my senses first, compelling my mind to blank out. I slowly withdrew and watched him compose himself with effort.

'I think we ought to go home.' My voice seemed to belong to someone else.

When we reached home, he stopped at my door.

'Thanks for everything, Disha. Please sleep in until late this once. You'll need it. I'll see you in the morning.'

It was me who turned and went in wordlessly.

13

Leaving on a Jet Plane

I recall the first time I saw the cameras for our film, they'd brought on an inexplicable sinking sense of dismay. We'd reached the studios a little before seven that morning, battling sleep and a nip in the moist breezes that augured rain by mid-morning. As the van was unloaded, the equipment seemed all dauntingly huge and formidable. With their appearance the movie ceased to be a topic of discussion and had moved into the realm of realities.

I have the greatest respect for actors. What they seem to pull off daily with consummate ease is a talent that I am most deficient in. To ease us all in, Amit initiated a series of small rehearsals that ran us through the entire sequence. Not that I was expected to act or anything. Just speak or respond to what were in reality fairly simple questions. During the run-through, I'd warmly respond and give cogent replies to all that was asked. But the simple act of switching the camera on had me freeze. Fortunately, the first runs seemed to confirm that I had fairly decent screen presence. I hoped what it meant was that a mumble and the attempt at a smile would pull me through.

A movie set, even one that is midway between a feature and a documentary like this, which borrows heavily from previous footage, has one overwhelming demand. It demands that you wait. It demands you forage for scraps of patience within you. The processes are tedious. So many things need to be set up. So many times 'cut' needs to be called and then there's always a huddle that snowballs into a discussion if not a full-blown argument.

Thankfully, there is always music on the sets. If recorded music is unavailable, the guys just begin impromptu rehearsals or jam. In the few spaces of peace and quiet, I steal myself away to reminisce.

Often I think back to how music formed a bridge between my old life and new.

꼬

I had to locate the phone with considerable effort. The greyness and the misty atmosphere around indicated it was very early in the morning.

'Good morning, sleepyhead!'

'Why are you waking me up, Sid?'

'I'm sorry. Go right back to sleep after this. I just wanted to say goodbye.'

'Goodbye?'

'Yeah, I'm at the airport, ten minutes from boarding my flight to Delhi. Tony and Joe are on either side of me just to make sure I don't make a run for it. It looks like I'm being kidnapped by an international ring of criminals.'

I couldn't make sense of it. Sweeping cobwebs of sleep away, I sat up to understand him better.

'I'm joking about how bloody firang my brothers look next to my desi skin. Smile, Disha.'

'It's Disha? What are you doing waking her up this early after a concert?'

'Joe says hi!'

I responded with greater warmth to Joe. I would miss him.

'Disha says hi! Okay spare me your crosstalk, guys. Disha, some official work has come up. An important series of meetings in Delhi and thereabouts and the family has decided to send in the three musketeers this time.'

'How long will you be away?'

'They haven't told me. I know zilch about the background or my role. The flight has been earmarked as a briefing session and you should see how eagerly Tony is looking forward to the torture.'

'Poor you!'

'Poor me is right. I smoked only two joints last night, but it was major and I'm still pinning angel wings on every soul I see. I wish I was spared this.'

'You smoked up? Where's mine?'

I could hear him argue with Joe. The younger one could be quite a pain to deal with if he chose.

'You simply can't ask a respected, respectable older

brother this.'

'Respected, my left toe! I haven't had access to decent stuff in ages. How does it help to have the best lead guitar in all of India as a brother when I never have stuff passed on to me?'

'Drop dead, Joe. Let me just finish this call with Disha.'

I heard him arguing in the background and I heard his message for me.

'And, Disha, tell Sid to be half as nice to me as he is to you.'

'But Sid isn't ever nice to me!'

There was silence. I could hear faint puzzlement—even hurt—in it.

'I'm very nice to you, Disha. Always. Especially after I found out you are just a baby, younger than even Dave.'

'She's younger than Dave?'

'Okay, Joe. Butt off my conversation.'

But I was enjoying all the crosstalk, especially when Sid was being so human and engaging.

'Why is talking to Disha only your conversation?'

'Because I called her. You can call her too.'

'But the lady hasn't given me her phone number.'

'She hasn't given me her number either. She's in Lila's room so the number remains the same.'

Stunned silence. I thought it was cute though. So him.

'Dude, you have Lila's number?'

'Of course. Didn't you ever call her? Or Nina?'

'Ewww! You are a sick freak, Sid. Whoever calls sisters?'

'I'm sorry, Disha. Joe has no idea how close I am to fratricide. Make that multiple, now that Tony says hi!'

⁂

I couldn't go back to sleep after that. In the grips of a deep sense of misery, I had managed to calmly cater to each demand the extraordinary day had made of me yesterday. And now, finally, my mind was unfrozen and I was free to think, leaving the doors open for chaotic thoughts to flood me. The gang was just as intimidating as before in the absence of Joe, who by now I'd begun to suspect was really a big softie and a complete darling, if left to himself.

I think Ronny started it at dinner. 'Can I have a picture and an autograph please, Disha?'

All of them burst into laughter as I turned red.

'I wouldn't mind a pin-up either.' This was Jimmy's contribution. And then all of them stared at me with wide and fake adoring eyes.

'What are you all talking about?' Jayashree asked irritably.

'You missed it, Joy to the World! We are now in the exalted presence of a true-blue star.'

Jayashree looked puzzled. No way in her view could anyone fit that bill.

'And, man, was she hot!'

'What kind of talk is that?' Aunty Shubhra reprimanded. She turned and looked at me kindly. 'You really sounded beautiful and you looked the part too. Ignore these rowdies.'

The uncles graced us with their presence, resulting in

mildly better behaviour.

'But, Aunty, you've got to admit there was sizzling chemistry between Nishith and Disha. As guardians, you lot ought to ask Disha what that was all about.'

No one asked me but there was an expectant silence. I laughed. 'Nishith is the most private and hands-off guy in the band. That was an act. He's a performer.'

'Besides, dude, if she were to go out with someone from the band, it would only be Sid.'

'Wouldn't you? She knows him best of all. He is the best musician in the band, the best-looking and alpha male types, too. And through all this, Sid has been her sugar daddy. Don't tell me you haven't noticed?'

I didn't want to but ended up noticing Aunty Karen's forehead creasing up. I leaned towards the gang. 'Thanks for taking such a keen interest in my interests! When there is someone significant, I will be the first to let you know. Till then, can we please, please switch off all the speculation. Thank you!'

The older set seemed amused. 'That's what eight thousand screaming fans dying to kiss your feet do to your ego.'

'Eight thousand minus six.'

'Which six?'

'Us six.'

'No, I am sure dying to kiss Disha's feet.'

And there was more teasing and laughter. Thankfully, the momentary amusement I provided was fickle and they sped on to other avenues. 'Disha, I didn't know you don't have a cell phone,' Amulya Uncle mentioned just as we were all winding up the meal. Everyone at the table was quiet. Phones were venerated.

I was compelled to answer. 'I don't need one. I don't have any friends here. And I rarely go out.'

'Today, a cell phone is a necessity. You must tell Karen or me or anybody here for that matter, if there are things you need. Always remember you are one of our kids now. I didn't know till Sid told me this afternoon.'

'What did Sid say?' Aunty Karen asked.

'They were filling me in on how their meeting had gone at around four this afternoon. Sid reminded me to get Disha a cell phone because in his absence the band has no other way to keep in touch with her. And I am happy because in any case I wanted to get her something nice to mark her debut last night.' Uncle smiled. He was in a reminiscent mood.

'After college, Chittaranjan and I both joined this government office together, as clerks. I was amazingly complacent with my seventeen-hundred-rupee salary and worked hard to spend it all on foolish things.'

'Seventeen C bucks?'

'Yes, it seemed like a kingly sum in those days.'

'You won't get even a month's worth packets of cigs with that money now.'

'Don't remind me how much I pay for all your vices. Back then, Chittaranjan saved each paisa over two years. He had the clearest head for finance and economics I've ever seen. It was Chittaranjan who set up our business and it was he who taught me the ropes as his junior partner, patiently instilling financial discipline in me.'

'You are still not disciplined financially,' one of his brothers pointed out rather helpfully.

'I know. But whatever little I am, it was through Chittaranjan's acumen. Then Disha, maybe five years after your birth, your ma began to have terrible asthma complications and the doctors advised fresh air, away from the fumes and the humidity of Kolkata. Do you know what he did?'

'What?' Dave asked.

'He just handed over the business to me. It was worth lakhs by then. But he just gave it to me saying he preferred to start afresh in Hamirpur where both of us had grown up.'

'No one gives away stuff worth lakhs!'

'I know. But that's who Disha's dad was. And in and around Hamirpur, he started, I think, in all maybe seven cooperative enterprises—weaving, oil mill, milk, pottery, carpentry and such stuff. And because of his vision each of them is still financially viable. I think in each he maintained a very small stake, maybe 5 per cent or less, which I guess is now Disha's and her sisters'. But given how successful they are, I guess even that would be huge. That's Chittaranjan for you!'

Jayashree had a pertinent question. She always did. 'Then why does she need you to buy her a phone?'

'She doesn't need me to. I consider it a privilege that I get to do something small for Chittaranjan's daughter.'

As dinner was being wound up, Sadhan was delegated

to fetch the phone. 'Al, Sid wanted you to teach Disha the operational basics for the phone.'

Al, the resident tech wizard, looked at the case. 'You got her an iPhone?'

'Why, is it bad?'

'No, Uncle. It's my dream phone. And it is way beyond what I can afford.'

'I could get you one. But, Al, there are eight of you, not counting Nina. I'd just go bankrupt.'

'I'll just have to find a rich woman to marry,' Al muttered. He thought for a moment and then he turned to me with a wicked smile. 'Oh lovely Disha, will you marry me? I just need this phone as dowry.'

'What you'll get is a spanking from me,' Aunty Parul warned, holding her head. 'They'll drive us all mad.'

It was a patently heartbroken Al who came with me to my room to educate me. He plonked on my bed and looked around. 'What an ugly room!'

'It's nice,' I defended.

'Lila is creepy. You are not. You can't really like this room.'

He took the phone out of its packaging and held it reverently in his hand. 'I can't believe I'm holding this only to hand it over to a tech-illiterate babe. There isn't a god!'

'You could marry the phone,' I suggested.

'I already have, a million times in my dreams.'

Then, he began to concentrate on the phone and twiddled with a lot of buttons before getting down to business. 'See here, this icon, the one that looks like a blurb in a cartoon?

That is your message app. And this red dot tells you there's a message waiting so you need to click here to see it.'

It read:

Quit gaming and teach her only the basics.

'And this is how you reply.'

He slowly took me through the buttons. He typed out a series of expletives and sent it. A reply came immediately.

Disha, did you like the phone? For the record, your no. is 98330 4251*. Am sending you all the guys' nos. now.

I shortly received four business cards, which Al showed me how to save. 'Do you have Sid's number?' I thought he kept his voice extra casual.

'No, not really.'

He then showed me how to save the number from an SMS.

14

Creep

It felt as if I was cold all the time. Like there was a piercing wind that froze my insides, but no one else around felt a thing. At night, in the tundra of my room, the bleakest loneliness welled up like an illness. I refused to diagnose what it was.

Vidyut called a couple of days later.

'Hello! Hope you are fine. Disha, we are meeting for a practice session at three this afternoon. Can you make it?'

I hesitated and then confessed. 'Sid took me around. I don't know the city at all.'

'That's not an issue. I'll come and pick you up and drop you back too. Not later than seven thirty.'

On the way, Vidyut filled me in. There was a two-day rock festival in Chandannagar. The organizers were a bunch of young professionals and college students who had worked tirelessly to find sponsors and to bring live rock music into the lives of other enthusiasts and hoped to convert some of the uninitiated too. We were the closing act of the show, the last band to take the stage on the second day.

'We need to expand our repertoire with you. The plan is to have another two songs and then build from there. So you need to come up with two compositions that you are completely at ease with and we'll refine a set around them.'

Vidyut spoke all the way. It was pleasant to have a conversation and to have someone point out places of interest as we went. Those same streets I had ridden down on now seemed to come alive with history and interest. Of course, his list was heavy on nondescript outlets, which offered manna in the form of samosas or roshogollas. On the flip side, I had still not shortlisted the two songs by the time I reached the practice hall.

Ashraf and Shady greeted me, the latter quite enthusiastically. Nishith didn't, though he shot me a long, silent look. While they were setting up, I hurriedly identified the two songs I wanted to bring to the band. My first pick was a unique-sounding taranā in Rāg Kāmod and the best thing about this composition was that it permitted endless possibilities of playing around with its tāl or beat.

All of them seemed to appreciate its richness, depth and versatility immediately, and I sang it again, with Vidyut accompanying me faintly on the drums. When I paused after the sthāyi or the fixed initial verse of the composition, he played out small groups of beats and pauses that complemented and elaborated upon the beat progressions within the song.

The other was a rāg pradhān, a pure rāg-based composition, almost like a madhya laya khayāl but in Bangla. This was simple, meaningful and melodic; its lyrics asking a lady why tears brimmed in her eyes, set in Rāg Madhuvanti.

The entire frame would be created and fully defined only after Sid joined us. I had introduced the vocal part and the composition to all of them. They would now come back with ideas on how to adapt it best to the fusion they hoped to present on stage.

꧁꧂

What amazes me about Juhi is how effortlessly she morphs into a creature of grace, beauty and immense poise when the cameras roll. It is the same Juhi in many ways, yet with the rough edges and her mildly petulant ways so beautifully controlled and hidden. This was only a dry run, so she had pitched it midway, somewhere between boredom and doing her job for the day.

'From all you have told us, it is clear that your closest relation within the band is with Sid. What about the others? Do you share a rapport with them all?'

'She loves me the most!' Nishith quips. 'High time you declared it, Disha.'

That provokes a mild battle between a loudly protesting Shady and him.

'Can't keep this hidden any longer, D. You have to declare your love for me in public. Now.'

Param though passing by catches it all and flashes an indulgent smile with a mere touch of inquisitiveness.

'So who is it really, Disha?'

☙

Sid was not back for our next practice session either. All of them wanted me to sing each song twice as they listened carefully the first time and then taped it on their phones to help familiarize so they could construct and renovate the basic scheme later. Then, I sat on the floor like the ardent fan I was fast transforming into while they rehearsed three songs from their repertoire that I had not heard before. After multiple renditions of each, replete with small conferences and corrections and new collaborations that they decided to run by Sid, it was time for a break.

Nishith came and lay down beside me, face down, on his folded arms. Shady and Ashraf left the room, as did Vidyut to organize snacks, tea and cigs. They were all back when Nishith turned and now lay staring at me, almost unblinking, for an uncomfortably long time.

'There's something intriguing about you.'

Ashraf was at his keyboard by now and had just touched the keys with a couple of faint plink sounds. 'Leave her alone.'

'Since when have you been interested in girls, Ashraf?'

His face went red. 'Disha is Sid's girl,' he elaborated carefully.

It was Vidyut who reacted, 'No, she's not!'

Ashraf began to play softly. As if it was imperative he

had clarity Vidyut sought to probe.

'Why did you think she is?'

Ashraf chose to ignore him.

Dee dee did did dum dee dee boop did
Dee dum dee did did boop-boop dum

'Heck man, Sid doesn't talk to her or even look at her!' Vidyut persisted.

Shady was the one who pointed it out. 'And since when is that normal for Sid?'

'You know, it can also mean that he has nothing in common with her.'

'Or?' Shady persisted.

'What do you think, Ashraf?' Vidyut wanted to know.

Dee do bop bop did did dum dee dee

Shady chose to answer. 'Oh, I think Sid is totally in love with Disha. He doesn't see her like he does all those other chicks he never goes anywhere with; would never have brought her to the band otherwise. And the way he is around her. I can't imagine you haven't figured it out too, Vidyut. It's out there, man. Very obvious.'

I sat there, trying my best to ignore this conversation had anything to do with me.

'For me, that doesn't matter in the least.' That drawl was Nishith's. All eyes, except mine, turned to him for clarification.

'I love being the other guy in a gal's life. You get the

confidence, the tenderness, all the desires and loving, without the dumb headache of maintaining a relationship with her.'

'Too bad it isn't official with Sid yet, Disha, or you couldn't have resisted taking up Nishith's stepney offer,' Shady volunteered with a grin.

'You can act as sassy as you like, Shady. But dude, I know I'm right.'

There was silence. And he still lay indolently, looking up at me.

'Do you know who's the best I've had and the most unerringly reliable?'

The guys waited for him to add. 'There's this relative of mine, a cousin's wife. You all know I don't even recall how many people actually live in that rambling old animal farm of a family home of ours, it's that chaotic. But man, is life there interesting! She's forty-one now and brings me experience, gratitude, freedom and a regular reliable source. I'm a happy fulfilled man with no headaches.'

'It sounds horribly illicit.'

'That's all in the head. In reality these tags don't mean shit.'

'So how did it start?'

'Way back in the mists of antiquity. I must have been about fifteen then.'

'What about the rest of the family? Won't they figure it out?'

'Do I care?'

'And her husband, your cousin?'

'I'm not the one married to him. He's her headache, not mine.'

'Okay, guys, let's change the topic. We are no longer just a bunch of jerks these days.'

Ashraf felt enough crap had been spoken in my presence. But I did join in the conversation then.

'If you were just fifteen then, Nishith, you were being molested.'

This was something he had never considered; I could tell by his quizzical expression.

'Are you out of your mind? Guys don't get molested.'

'Dude, they do.'

'I don't know which guy would. I'm not one of them.'

'Let's do the math. She was twenty-nine then.'

'So? It was the best thing that could have happened to me. Buggers, it still is!'

'Ease off, Nishith. Some of us find such things disgusting.'

Nishith looked at Ashraf with hard eyes. Changing tack, he went swiftly into attack mode. 'It's no more disgusting than your sweet crush on Shady.'

'Shady is my best friend. Why should that disgust you?'

'It's not the friendship part. It's the can't-keep-hands-off-each-other, which is.'

I had never seen this form of a schism in this group. The conversation was rapidly degenerating. 'Just because you are a perv doesn't mean everyone else in the world is.'

'I prefer being a perv to being closet gay.'

Ashraf's voice was so cool I could tell he was very

offended. 'Some of us can handle our sexuality without being crazy and overt.'

Shady alone seemed untouched by the simmering tension and laughed hard. 'Chill man, Ashraf. You know Nishith will say anything for effect.'

Nishith sat up beside me, his knees all over the place and he looked at me with penetrating eyes now. 'This thing with Sid, it could just be proximity and hormones. You don't know what temptation an unrelated woman in the same house presents.'

15

The Boys are Back in Town

Strangely, that was the first thought that came to my mind when I found Sid at Sunday breakfast. I had blanked out the conversation, choosing not to even think about the guys' speculation of Sid's probable feelings for me. I just withdrew, somehow scared, affected by it all.

Technically, the household's Sunday brunch could put a full-fledged lunch to shame with the table creaking with food, raucous conversation and everyone inclined to linger forever. As I entered the hall, I noticed more heads than usual and I identified Sid by the way he sat, his back to the doorway. His mother had engaged him in an exclusive conversation. She wanted to know about Delhi and his experiences there—the work and what he did with his off-duty time.

'You get to be my driver and escort today. I have church in about forty-five minutes. Then I need to visit Renu. There's a bit of shopping I need your help with. And it would be nice to catch a coffee somewhere.'

'Spare him today, Karen. Take Biren or any of the boys

instead. They all drive well. Poor Sid is likely exhausted with all the work and travel. He should just have a lazy day at home to unwind,' his dad countered.

'No, Biren won't do. Sid is mine, too. If he can rush off to Delhi at your bidding for eight days, he jolly well can spend a day with me without you objecting.'

'I wasn't objecting. And he didn't rush to Delhi at my bidding. Our clients specifically asked for him at the meetings. He somehow seems to strike a chord with them. And now he needs his rest too.'

'Not an issue, Dad. I'll come, Ma,' he smiled at her. 'Just don't overdo the shopping bit.'

༄

I was in bed with a book fairly late at night. I tried to read, but every so often, I would find myself wandering into a haze. A strange disquiet flitted through me, prompting introspection. It was noble of Amulya Uncle to have brought me to Kolkata and to have given me a place to stay in his own house, shielding me from an uncertain future at Hamirpur. I tried to pretend the best I could that nothing had changed. But my life had. Who I was, had. How the people around perceived me, had. Of everything that concerned me, I had lately realized how truly alone I now was. And this life I led, it wasn't me. It wasn't anything my life had prepared me for. I wasn't equipped to live among almost-strangers, dependent on their goodness and mercy. The impossibility to opt for a change gnawed at me.

There was a faint knock at my door. I had bolted it for the night. Opening the door revealed Sid—solemn, distant.

'Would you have a minute?'

I stared at him, partly in dismay, his absence having made him a stranger to me now, and I felt the uncertainty return. I moved out of the way half-heartedly.

'I just wanted to give you this. It's something I picked up in Delhi.'

It was a paper bag so chic and unexpected I took it from him with nerveless fingers.

'We have two shows coming up. My designer friend in Delhi, Teju, rustled up something to save me the headache of costume-hunting at the last minute.'

The actual parcel was tied with string and I picked at the knots. There were two outfits. They were both so exquisite I realized I'd never seen anything like them. One was a black raw-silk kurta beautifully stitched with wide raglan sleeves and deep slits at the sides. The salwar was sea-green and closely pin-tucked so that it looked rich and unique. The other was a faintly embroidered cream ensemble with a short kurta and an ornate Patiala salwar topped off with a soft georgette dupatta. I touched the beautiful fabric in awe. His words were whispers, 'So you like them?'

I nodded, my throat too dry.

'Why haven't you spoken to me at all today, Disha? Or all this time I was away and you had my phone number.'

I hesitated, 'I thought you were busy.'

'You could have at least said hi at breakfast.'

There was silence for a while. Nothing I could bring myself to say would suffice.

'We have a very busy three weeks ahead of us.'

'I know.'

'So if I don't say something, you won't speak at all.'

'It's not that.'

'Then what is it?'

There was no way I could tell him what I now knew.

'I just have nothing to say.'

'I don't know any woman who is ever at a loss for words.'

'You know a lot of women, don't you, Sid?'

'Depends on what you mean by "know".'

I refused to elaborate. If I close my eyes now, I can still see his expression as he folded the dresses back with care and placed them on the pillow. He sat for a long minute looking down and then went to the door.

'The worst part about being in Delhi was not seeing you.'

I looked at him, mute, really wishing he would never say things like that to me.

☙

When I went to the terrace to pick up my clothes, Sid and Nina were talking earnestly and both turned to look at me, unsmiling. Then, Sid's features softened.

'Disha, come here.'

He bent to kiss me on my cheek as a greeting. By Nina's eyes, I knew she had seen the flush on my face—this greeting was still too new, Sid still overpowering.

'We have a practice session at six thirty.'

He slid an easy arm around my shoulders and held me there. 'We could do with your advice too.'

'Please, Sid. In a household like ours it is better for her not to know.'

'You know who Disha is.'

She lapsed into silence. He turned to me. 'Help us out here. This is about Nina's marriage.'

'Why are you telling me this?'

'I need your counsel. We both do. So there is Nilanjan Chakraborty, one of Nina's closest friends since her schooldays. They've only been friends so far. But Nina thinks she has the most comfort with him. She wants to explore, to see if anything could work out with him.'

'Then she should.'

Nina turned to me, 'It's not that easy. He comes from a very traditional, virtually orthodox family.'

'Nina is a true-blue Bengali in every way. But it won't pass his family's notice that her mother is British and she looks it.'

'Perhaps as he and his family get to know you better, these things won't matter so much.'

Her voice was sadly bitter. 'To his family, it always will.'

'And Nina just doesn't have the time. Now there is Sudipto Ganguly.'

'Who is he?'

'This guy is a relative of one of Ma's friends. Born and brought up in Toronto and completely Canadian in every way. Has an excellent career in Kolkata now and loves it here. He has seen pictures of Nina and would marry her tomorrow if we said yes.'

'I see.'

'The family feels Sudipto is too good to pass up just on a whim. It's even uncertain Nilanjan has those feelings for Nina, and if he does, he would ever follow through.'

I turned to Nina. 'What do you want to do?'

She stayed silent, not meeting my eyes.

'I would opt for Nilanjan too,' I told her.

'Why?' Sid demanded to know.

'Because Nina cares for him. And Sudipto, for all his eligibility, is merely a passing stranger.

16

Hello, I Love You, Won't You Tell Me Your Name?

Sid was right. It was a very hectic period for us. The practice sessions were exhausting now that Sid's presence had the focus back squarely on the music. The guys gossiped or sniped far less. I noticed that Vidyut seemed to watch Sid more carefully, particularly when he was around me. And Nishith had somehow gotten into the habit of talking to me a lot. While the others tinkered with their instruments, he'd sit talking to me in a low voice about a whole lot of unrelated, almost incomprehensible, experiences and thoughts.

Composing my two songs into a complete arrangement was harder than I'd imagined. During that process, I realized what gifted musicians all of them were and just how serious and meticulous they were about their craft. Each session meant constant sharpening of their skills. Sid's suggestion was that we work hard on the taranā for the Chandannagar concert where I would repeat my bhātiyāli and introduce the new format. And for the Kharagpur concert which was later and afforded us more practice I could present the same tarānā and then introduce the rāg pradhān.

We practised over and over, often exhausting ourselves completely. One such evening, well after eleven in the night, Sid and I got stuck in a huge traffic snarl. We found a minor road as diversion and then just like that we stopped at a tea stall outside a large deserted parking lot. Both of us were tired and hungry despite the fact that we'd eaten pizzas around nine.

'Excuse me, I hope you don't mind the intrusion.'

Sid looked over at the bespectacled young man without curiosity. He seemed more than a little shy and flustered. 'It's just that you seem extremely familiar, like I know you from somewhere.'

We still waited for him to ask us something.

'May I know your name please? It would help.'

'Siddhant Banerjee,' Sid volunteered. The young man thought it over and then shook his head.

'No, doesn't ring a bell. May have seen you at a wedding or something.'

He turned to me. 'Sorry, ma'am.' It was an effort to smile. He went away to claim his clay pot of masala tea and came back hopefully.

'Are you some stars or something? Famous?'

Now Sid just gave him a dull stare. A teenager in baggy shorts came over to hand us our cups of tea where we sat on a worn sun-bleached wooden bench. As I reached for it, Sid decided to elucidate, louder for the young man to hear.

'And ma'am here is Disha Ray Chaudhuri.'

'Oh man! You are Sid and Disha from Dreams!' He was blathering. 'I am a fan. A huge fan. I recognized you. It's just I didn't expect to see you here. Like this. And you are stars. You are the best guitarist there is, Sid! I mean it.'

Sid's question sounded serious. 'Do you have a phone with a camera?'

The guy looked puzzled. 'Yes, I do.'

'Then you can click away. Only don't take any of Disha's solo. Her boyfriend is awfully possessive.'

I gave him a weird look. He grinned back at me, happy at his stupid joke.

༄

'So who is my jealous boyfriend?'

He looked at me, his eyes naughty. 'Why? Do you really want young men carrying your picture around?'

'How does it matter? If he wanted to, he could take it off the stage.'

'I am miffed actually. He only recognized me in association with you. A twelve-year career and a one-gig-old babe upstages me.'

I knew he was joking.

'Yeah, call yourself Siddhant and even your mother won't recognize you.' I immediately sobered, 'I shouldn't have mentioned your mom. I won't again.'

'And you aren't sorry for stealing my limelight?' He was mock annoyed.

'Disha is an unusual name. I think he needed that to put two and two together. And he didn't rave about me as a musician, though he called you the best guitarist there is.'

'I'm sure he's as good a judge of that as he is with recognizing faces.'

These moments were too few, moments when he remained playful and unguarded. Our ease with each other was built on moments like these. I wanted to hold on to their promise.

'Does this happen to you often, Sid?'

'What, being upstaged by a babe? Never!'

'Being recognized by strangers on the streets... It felt scary in a way.'

'Not too often. Get used to it, Disha.'

꩜

One night after a particularly gruelling session that went on late into the night, I fell asleep in the soothing silence of the car. Sid woke me up as he parked. 'Wake up, sleeping beauty! We are home.'

I blinked at him, wishing fervently he would just let me be. Then out of the mists of sleep, I made a weird connection. 'I think Annette is very beautiful.'

I turned my large sleepy eyes at him. 'Your girlfriend.' Sleep closed my eyes to muse some more.

'You were kissing her on the evening of our concert.'

'Is that all you remember about the evening of our concert?'

I nodded, my head finding a comfortable bump at the edge of the headrest. An insistent thought made me open my eyes to look at him balefully. 'Let me sleep.'

He pushed my hair back from my face.

'Just two minutes more.'

Sid practically had to drag me upstairs. On the landing of the first floor, we ran into his parents as they were coming out of the hall, probably after watching TV. His dad looked at the two of us. 'Sid, I think you are pushing Disha too hard. It's too soon to.'

I yawned—it was uncontrollable.

'I never liked the idea of her joining the band. Clearly, she is finding the going impossible,' his mother observed.

'She is in the band now. Like it or find it tough, she stays. She really has no exit option.'

Aunty persisted, 'She isn't your lead singer. And she's only done one show.'

'You won't understand, Ma.'

'So explain it to me. Why of all the thousands of girls you have access to, it has to be only her?'

'None of the thousand girls matter, none came home to stay.'

'Is that what this is?' Aunty challenged him.

'Yes, Ma. When someone lives with you, they are family. And that's what families do. Look out for each other's best interests. Create opportunities. Make sure nothing and nobody harms or ill-treats them.'

'I think, Sid, your loyalties are misplaced.'

'I could say the same about your hostility.'

I had broken out of his grip and had sat down on the stairs, too sleepy to comprehend what was unfolding around me.

'Take Disha to bed, Sid,' Amulya Uncle directed.

Sid turned to me. Even half passed out, I sensed he was somehow defeated, sad. 'You can sleep on the stairs now if you want to.'

I continued sitting, leaning my barely sentient head against the wall. In a minute, he was back.

'Okay, Disha. Point made. Point taken. Let's just get you to bed.'

I didn't move. My eyes closed.

'You do realize I'm sleepy and dead tired too.'

That woke me up. I looked at Sid, and in the oblique lights of the stairwell landing, his eyes looked obscure and yet deep somehow. I held out a palm. For a while, he didn't take it and I expected he was going to tell me something. Instead, he bent to help me up. I stood up now and slowly went up the stairs, thankful that he was supporting me.

17

Knocking on Heaven's Door

I didn't quite realize when the band and its rhythms completely took over my days. I recall very clearly Aunty Karen was not very pleased to be informed that we would be spending two nights at Chandannagar. She didn't conceal the fact that she found my proximity to Sid unacceptable. It ran as a strong thread through all my interactions with her in the household.

'I'm used to you touring, Sid. I'm not sure she should be going along too. I'm not sure rock festivals are apt places for women.'

'But Disha will be with Sid throughout,' his dad pointed out. 'Sid, you understand, I hope, that she's your responsibility. Take special care.'

Sid was looking at his mother. 'I promise I'll be back for lunch on Sunday. And, Ma, I'll go with you for the evening mass at church. Just the two of us.' Then he turned to Nina. 'Will you be alright?'

The rest of the breakfast was hijacked by the guys' loud

discussion on whether it made sense to make a trip out of it and land up for the concert in Chandannagar or to do their usual Saturday night pub crawl instead.

Aunty Parul was curious. 'You are a mob of six. Do women even glance your way at places like that?'

'We have our bait!'

'What bait?'

'So Joe puts on this massive American drawl and we stand around trying hard to act like software guys with a Yank business associate. Works like magic.'

'No, it doesn't. Because our man Joe invariably has something to say in his worst Bāngāl accent and the game goes up in smoke.'

Joe was laughing heartily, 'Of course, the look on the chicks' faces is priceless.'

'Once, we even managed to get past it by convincing the bimbettes that he was a billionaire philanthropist with a keen interest in helping the poor and disenchanted in Bangladesh, where he unfortunately also picked up these strange phrases.'

'You boys are all crooks!'

'We have a lot of fun, Ma. And in the end that's all that matters.'

Aunty Shubhra looked thoughtful. 'Parul, don't you think we should start looking for girls for the twins?'

Her tentative suggestion was drowned out in loud protests. No matrimony seemed the reigning theme. There was cacophony for a while.

'See what you did to Tony. The poor man is finished!'

'What happened to Tony?' Jayashree's words were suspicious and sharp.

'No offence, Joy. But you do keep him on a very short leash. The bloke is whipped.'

The chatter turned into reminiscences of the pre-Joy era in Tony's evolution when his shirts were jaunty and a twinkle sat like fire in his eye.

'And to think at one time he almost outdid Sid.'

'No one, no one ever, came close to outdoing Sid. But yeah, the man had a life, and nice women to hang around with.'

'R.I.P., Tony!'

Tony himself sought refuge in stony silence.

The Chandannagar experience marked an extremely important milestone in my progression as a musician. It was my first outstation show and that was when I experienced the hospitality loving organizers extend to artistes they invite. Besides, I was travelling with the band and while everyone else seemed to accept it as normal, I still needed to pinch myself to believe all of it was really happening.

We met up early at Vidyut's and then began our drive. Ashraf and Shady wanted to go on their bikes. Nishith went in Vidyut's van while Sid took me with him.

'I've been meaning to ask you. Didn't you feel any stage fright at all during the first performance? You were surprisingly confident and cool.'

'I'm used to it.'

'What, singing at rock shows?'

'No, singing to crowds. I've been singing at temple festivals at Hamirpur since the age of six, but devotional songs only.'

'Didn't an audience of mainly long-haired guys scare you?'

'I don't know if you'll understand. It is so deeply internalized that a part of me comes alive only during performances. That part takes over completely, almost beyond conscious effort. Yet, in a sense, that is me, all of me unleashed.'

The way he heard me out felt as if he knew what I was talking about.

'And that me is surer, confident, melodious and loves the adulation and the energy of it all. Do you understand, Sid?'

'In a way, I do. I call it the performer chromosome.'

That term I was unfamiliar with. Yet, I understood there was something deeper that held all of us together. Sid effortlessly volunteered information about his own journey.

'My uncle gave me a guitar for my twelfth birthday. I learnt a few chords from friends, but I sucked at it.'

'So, when did you get this good?'

'I don't know how it came about. There was this phase in my life where just two things mattered—football and my guitar.'

'No babes?' I teased him.

'Babes still don't matter, Disha. No matter what anyone tells you.'

Dreams and another band called Blueprint were given three double rooms each at a quiet guest house, spilling over with greenery. Then the organizers realized that they hadn't budgeted that the band had a female member and hastened to provide another room for me—a tiny single room on the second floor with a wide balcony filled with sunlight and potted plants.

After dumping our kits, we went over to the venue as the evening's soundcheck was underway, mainly to catch up. There were six bands in all. There were plenty of girls. I don't know whether girlfriends or groupies. I was the only one from a band. Here, I realized the world of rock bands is almost cliquey—everybody seemed to know each other.

There was lots of hugging and backslapping, and when the concert began, all the bands huddled together at the enclosed area up in front by the stage, their comments appreciative and very technical.

'So this is Disha.'

Vidyut turned to the guy. 'Hi, Mandy. Yeah, this is what we had all dreamed about—Disha.'

'I missed your Rock for All gig. I heard she's very raw, but passable.'

Nishith's arm brought me closer to him. 'Cut her a break, Mandy. Don't forget your first time. Bugger, I wondered how your college could have even let you represent it to the world outside. You sucked that bad, man!'

'She can't have had her first gig with Dreams!'

'She did. And she did great, go tell your informants that.'

Mandy turned his canny and thoughtful eyes at me.

'The only way that could happen is if she was Sid's protégé. But Sid would never risk a Dreams' performance.' He tried to sound flippant. 'So either Sid is bitten bad this time. Or Disha here is very good.'

Ashraf had his hands in his pockets. He was barely audible when he said, 'Or it could be both.'

The evening swept me away with its mix of sounds and contagious energy. In a short span, I had equipped myself to instinctively respond to this music though as a neophyte. The time I spent with the band was warm and intimate, like we were a family woven out of choice. And just as Nishith had protected me from Mandy's barbs, all of them formed a shield between the rest of the crowd and me, ensuring I stayed within their circle—often updating me on bands, their members, insider info on their USP and other hidden features, the sound system or the way the stage was set.

Only Sid went missing. He was more a flash seen in passing, either catching up with friends from other bands or conferring and spending time with the organizers. Often I'd see him with a different girl and each girl impeccably turned out, the kind whose looks and poise you see in glossies. After the show ended, all of us went backstage for a more private session of post-show socializing. The names and faces remain a whirl now yet the power of that unique confluence of music and bonhomie makes it all memorable. I was greeted with a great deal of warmth owed more to Dreams than to anything about me. At one point, Sid came up.

'The guys want to catch up and jam somewhere. And there'll be a whole lot of stuff you may not want to be around for.'

Already drooping from the exertions of my long day, I knew I didn't want any of it. While that social whirl was exhilarating, I didn't want to be around for the murkier stuff with strangers. I asked, almost a little unsure.

'Will an organizer take me back to the guest house?'

He gave me a 'don't-be-funny' look and led me away. Having observed that his social circuit was so large and impressive, I felt a little overwhelmed in his presence now. In the car, he spoke a tad too casually.

'I heard Mandy described you as raw.'

'His source has a good knowledge of music and an accurate reading of my skills.'

'He's someone whose opinions do not matter. And more importantly, whose opinion need not be trusted.'

'What do you mean?'

The eyes never wavered from the road ahead. Yet the slice of silence reminded me of the times he seemed to reconsider what he needed to say.

'There are rivalries between vocalists, between bands. Sowing seeds of doubt is part of the game. So it would be best to ignore him.'

❧

Preparing for bed in my room perched atop an empty house, my thoughts returned to Mandy's comments. I fidgeted with the tiny pot of night cream. Of course, each member of the audience would have an opinion, in fact, the less they knew about the music, the more vehement their opinions would be. A bent finger dabbed a dollop on my philosophizing nose. Didn't I have an opinion too? I went over my analysis of each singer I had heard that night, not on the basis of their musical abilities alone, but in every way.

It then struck me how superior the music of Derozio Dreams was—the reputation and respect certainly hadn't come undeserved. It had to do with the abilities of each person in the band. Further, it had to do with how simple and grounded as human beings they were and how it was all about coming together for the music, which to each of them was paramount, almost a religion.

Somehow, every vocalist I had heard this evening fell short of Nishith's electric persona and performance. On stage, he was uninhibited and open, almost wooing the crowds and asking for their love in return. He made a connection with the audience and his beautiful vocals only mirrored what was in his soul.

In contrast, I must have come off as immature and frightened, almost wary of being thrust into the arc lights. I realized it had less to do with my musical talents and more with my ease as a concert musician in this genre of music—it was mainly a mind thing. And I would have to do all it took to overcome it. These thoughts, cyclic and not all coherent, kept me awake for long. There was a light tap at the door and I froze. There was another tap. I approached the door.

'Sid, is that you?'

He didn't answer, but I knew it was him. The passage outside was pitch dark. It must have been very late.

'Were you asleep?'

'What's up, Sid?'

He didn't answer. I closed the door behind him.

'Is there something you needed to talk to me about?'

He located the door to the sit-out and let himself out. I followed and stood in the doorway, watching him look out into the dark beyond. In a while, he sat on the floor of the sit-out, his back propped against the wall. Apart from the many questions I'd probably never ask him, I found I hadn't anything to say to him either. It must have been almost an hour later of very warm, very intimate silence when I felt too drowsy to sit any more.

'I'm terribly sleepy, Sid.'

He looked at me, his head still against the wall as he did.

'Go to bed.'

Instead, I leaned forward to rest my head against him and stayed there, curled. His warmth held me close, his face shielding mine. That feeling caressed me as I drifted into sleep.

18

Black Magic Woman

The question put to me by Zubin in the course of that evening's shoot was simple.

'How difficult is it to be a woman in a rock band?'

❧

It was almost déjà vu. Just as our soundcheck was about to begin, a group of four ladies came up to meet Sid. Among them was this tall beauty with heavily streaked hair and amazing make-up, rich plum lipstick that matched perfectly with her tight black jumpsuit.

They hugged in mutual delight. And when he bent to kiss her on each cheek, I had to look away. I think I concentrated so hard on not noticing Sid with all the women that I noticed my surroundings only when someone spoke out my name on the powerful sound system.

'And this is for you, Disha.'

I looked up to find Nishith's eyes holding mine even as

his fingers held the mike up to sing.

> Now this mountain I must climb
> Feels like a world upon my shoulders
> Through the clouds I see love shine
> It keeps me warm as life grows colder
>
> In my life there's been heartache and pain
> I don't know if I can face it again
> Can't stop now, I've travelled so far
> To change this lonely life

I knew Nishith had a powerful voice, but this tender, mellifluous rendition was a surprise. I didn't know the song at all but the way he sang it, it sounded familiar and very meaningful. And I stood there, touched by the beauty of the moment.

'Disha, you go next,' Vidyut called out to me.

I half-turned to look at Sid. But he was absorbed in his companions. As I passed Nishith on the stairs up to the stage, he stopped to hug me lightly. It felt good, but I drew away quickly, aware that from him I was just seeking consolation from my own heartache and pain.

✥

I knew Sid was somewhere to my left at the back. But every note I sang, I sang for him, as if every member of the audience was just a fragment of him. I realized at the first concert, too, I had been only conscious of Sid and had sung to him alone.

But this was different. This time I had truly seen higher highs than before and had known the lowest lows as well. And my voice, my song and my feelings conveyed that. There was resounding applause and when it died down, I was surprised to find Sid close beside me.

'Just a minute, Disha.'

And his fingers wrapped around mine to raise my mike. 'Do we have Kaushik in the audience tonight?'

A young man wearing a short-sleeved T-shirt over a long-sleeved checked shirt leapt onto the stage. 'Hi! Why don't you do your thing?' Sid spoke into the mike.

The crowd cheered. Nishith brought his mike to the boy. I was told later what he did was called beatboxing. He took up a rhythm that was very catchy. In a couple of rounds, Nishith accompanied him with notes.

Sid turned to me. 'Your turn, Disha.'

And I launched into a swift ālāp overlay. Slowly, the band came in one by one for a spontaneous ten-minute jam session. That it was completely impromptu seemed to have been grasped by the audience and they listened mesmerized. This unrehearsed act actually tested our skills, our coordination and the maturity of all of us as a band, to the limits. I was just thankful I didn't drop the ball.

'Please join us in a huge round of applause to Kaushik, our man from Chandannagar!' Nishith urged the audience.

Kaushik look dazed and blissful while Nishith announced a five-minute break. Backstage, I went numb. Honestly, I was a little nervous singing a tarānā after this. I needn't have worried. It may have been the anxiety alone, but I did manage to bring it. And live in this magical night with a stupendous sound system, I felt the band had surpassed my expectations of how it would sound.

The crowd was ecstatic. And finally, when the entire concert came to a close, there were desperate pleas for encores. The band obliged and then Sid did a bluesy guitar solo that almost lapsed into an exploration of jazz. Each person in the vast audience stayed on until the festival had to be declared over. Ashraf dropped me back to the guest house on his bike, saying that the rest of them would take a lot longer to pack up. As I sat in my tiny room, I subconsciously kept an ear out for when they would all return. About half an hour later, I went down to the first floor. I heard voices. Ashraf opened the door to let me in.

'Hey come in. We are all celebrating,' Vidyut called out.

'Join the party.' Nishith poured something into a paper cup and brought it to me. 'Here's something you need. Something that will help you unwind and relax, make you comfortable in your own skin.'

'I'm sorry, Nishith. I'll have to pass.'

I searched the room for Sid. 'Could I please speak with you?'

But he was drinking deeply from his bottle as if he hadn't heard me. I waited.

'Go to sleep now, Disha. I'll talk to you in the morning.'

Shady spoke up, alcohol-fumed and loud, resuming a conversation I seemed to have interrupted. 'Boss, you can't have a flock of babes lined up in Chandannagar as well.'

Sid ignored him to take a deeper gulp out of his bottle.

'Now I begin to suspect you pay people to come and provide you the publicity.'

'Not at all. Paromita was in college with me, a good friend.'

'We went to the same college too. Why don't your hot college friends find us?'

An argument broke out then.

'Depends on whether you knew them in college.'

'No, depends on how you play the guitar.'

'Man, admit it. You are not Sid.'

I stood amidst all of it uncertainly. I knew Sid had refused to talk to me. I slowly left the room and went to back to mine.

⁂

It took me a while to emerge from the coils of sleep. I lay blinking in the dark, one factoid after another swimming into my ken—I was in the guest house, the concert was done, and this was Sid. I tried to focus on him but neither the dark nor my sleep-blurred eyes would let me. He was sitting at the edge of the bed.

'You wanted to speak to me.'

I struggled to sit up, but I couldn't speak. We had both moved to each other. A hand cupped my face. I wished I could see his, but the dark obliterated everything. His other hand caressed my shoulder with tentative fingertips. And somehow, all that I had stored inside of me, of having missed him so relentlessly for long, all the turbulent thoughts that raged since the night of my maiden concert flooded into me.

The kiss was just a feather touch. I was afraid to breathe, completely lost in this rapture and that feeling of being at peace. There was something sweet and unsure about Sid tonight. I knew it in the way he held me and how his fingers went over my back—asking, happy, mine. I felt it in his lips as they took turns at being uncontrolled and gentle. When we drew apart, he lay down and slowly pulled me down to him. We curled into each other, finding ways to absorb this togetherness—to celebrate, to give.

What I felt inside nearly choked me. It was intense. And irrational. It told me that every concern I had seen on Aunty Karen's face was justified. I couldn't have fallen more completely in love with Sid if I had tried. But apart for a little space on the fringes of his life as long as I stayed in his house, his life had simply no use for yet another woman. He had told me that often enough, indirectly. But right now, I simply had no defence against all the myriad responses that leapt in me at his touch. And more than anything else, I wanted him to know without being told what he had come to mean to me, and for this night to never end.

※

Sunlight tiptoes into rooms each morning—a different kind of lilting entry for each room. I often watched its shy entrance as mellow yellow hints tingeing the stark whites of the room I occupied. This morning, I was too exhausted by the events of the night to bear witness. Though I could tell that there was a flood of light from behind my eyelids.

'Wake up, sleepyhead.'

Something felt soothing, strongly comforting in a way I had never known. Then I woke up to the fact that I had been sleeping with my face buried in Sid's chest. It felt disorienting to have to draw away.

'And I'm the one who is supposed to have a hangover.' His eyes held a warm lazy smile.

'Do you?'

'No. Surprising, given the quantities of alcohol I'd drunk.'

'Were you drunk last night?'

'Like a fish. I remember the concert and then there is a sort of total blankness.'

I drew away from him, almost ashamed and guilty, as if I'd taken advantage of him when he was unconscious, unable to defend himself.

❧

'So what did you want to speak to me about?'

I had been absorbed in vacantly staring at the passing greenery, its beauty at odds with the unmanageable bleakness inside. I turned to Sid.

'I thought you were too drunk to remember anything.'

He shot me a searching look. 'Some recollections come through the haze.'

'I don't remember what it was now.'

19

Another Brick in the Wall

Nothing in life quite prepares us for what might hit us next. Often, each day feels like stepping off a cliff. We flail. We fall. We return, sometimes unhurt, to step off once more.

Our band practice sessions are known to be tight, efficient and productively coordinated. The film sets are fairly chaotic in contrast. Of course, the whole process of film-making is an amalgamation of diverse elements, and the numbers are practically unmanageable.

That Param and Amit have contrasting styles of functioning added substantially to the fragmentation of that narrative. Yet, not even the most acute of organizational skills can do much. It is almost noon and the succession of inane glitches had held up shooting. After much argument, it is decided to push lunchtime back to three and begin immediately. When called, Zubin is nowhere to be found. It is then that a distracted Amit informed us all that his permission to leave had been sought and granted. Param explodes. And a good fifteen minutes more are lost in the dust-up that follows; mostly Param letting off steam.

Amit brings it to a close with a quiet controlled statement. 'There are times when people need to leave, and whatever it does to your schedule, Param, they simply have to go. We've budgeted for it and we have to, at times, bow to the inevitable.'

A frenzied reorganization of the day's schedule and a surprisingly productive session thereafter ensure that quite a bit of progress is made despite. We soldier on until well past eight in the evening, tired, secretly hoping pack up would be declared soon. Param pulls out the phone from the pocket of his jeans, something he often does, especially when he needs to tell the time. He bends over the screen longer, as if reading. His voice sounds a little choked as he addresses us all.

'Some bad news, I'm afraid. It is a message from Zubin. Apparently his mother passed away this evening.' He shakes his head. 'I had no idea...'

Ashraf and I travel to Zubin's house in Vidyut's van. We talk a lot more than we normally do. Most of it is just disconnected thoughts in the form of empty chatter, as if to drown out the raw feeling of someone's absence. We find Sid waiting at the gates of the apartments for me.

'When I looked around for you they told me you'd already left with Vidyut. I'm sorry. I guess the news had us all disoriented.'

Zubin seems to be in a daze. He is dry-eyed and disbelieving. To each of us, he tries repeating the sequence of events as if attempting to redefine the outcome with each retelling.

Often, he asks perplexed. 'A fever, that's all it was. How can anybody die of just a fever?'

His older brother is still at the hospital trying to finish the formalities. A few relatives have come and an aunt even brings all of us tea, though none of us quite feel that refreshments are appropriate in this atmosphere of deep grieving. In a far corner, his ailing father sits in crumpled bedclothes, lost in a cocoon of his own memories. In the dry gloom of silences and the inadequacy of words, death seems so powerful, so close.

॰

We had been on the road for about an hour when Sid received a call and he stopped at the edge to take it.

'Hi, Nina. What's up?'

There was a long silence as he listened intently. His tone altered and he sounded tired the next time he spoke.

'I should be home in less than an hour and a half. We'll work something out. You should have called me immediately last night.'

Then, he sounded sad, 'Yeah, I was in concert then. I'm sorry, baby.' He put the phone away and sat, staring ahead.

'Has something happened?'

By then, he was busy dialling another number.

'What did you do, Ma? Were you just waiting for me to be out of the way to spring this?'

He seemed angrier as he listened. 'Yes, Disha is with

me and has been throughout. How does it matter to you or influence this senseless awful thing you have done?'

Thankfully, I couldn't hear the other side of this painful conversation.

'So do your worst to me. Why try and punish Nina by association? Why ruin her life in your prejudicial blindness?'

He listened some more.

'You know what, Ma. I'm done talking to you. No, you will not have a discussion with me when I come home. I don't want to ever talk to you again. And, Ma, congrats on your trophy of a Canadian son-in-law, no matter what it does to your daughter.'

He banged the phone down on the dashboard and rubbed his face in his palms. I wanted to speak but I dared not. I had understood roughly what had transpired, and his sorrow and anger were palpable.

He scrolled down to another number. 'Hey, Vidyut! I'm sorry, man. Something has come up. Some family matter, which means Disha and I need to rush home. Please tell the others too. Will call and plan sometime soon. No, nothing serious...just the usual irritating stuff. Take care.'

He didn't drive but sat looking adrift instead. When he looked at me, that beginning of a sad smile almost took my breath away as his left arm drew me to him. I went like metal scrap to a magnet. For a while, there was silence, and in that tranquil unspoken togetherness, both of us felt at peace.

'Ma has committed to Sudipto in such a public way that there is simply no turning back. And Nina seems devastated.'

Our togetherness in that moment seemed to grow and blossom until I could feel the return of the warmth from last night. His T-shirt had a guitar embossed on it and the tips of my fingers touched it lightly.

'Are you alright?'

'No, Disha. I had always believed we aren't really a family that forces its children into marriages of convenience. I just can't begin to comprehend this.'

'Parents make decisions based on the bigger picture.'

'I know. But all Nina was asking for was some time and preparedness.'

'You love her a lot, don't you?'

His arms tightened a little around me. Speaking about his feelings made him wary.

'You know, my family means the world to me. Of them all, I share the closest bond with Nina. God has been kinder to me by giving me the skin tone I have. Tony and Joe have always had trouble assimilating but it's always been the toughest on Nina, as she is a woman.'

'Is that why Nina is so quiet?'

'Partly. I would do anything for her happiness. And at this point, apart from breaking an almost engagement and creating a scene that may further impair Nina's chances, there is little I can do.'

'Perhaps the fact that you love her and will be there for her no matter what is the most important thing.'

'It can't be. I blame myself. I should have taken better care of her.'

'Women have sheltered lives, but their journeys are always tougher.'

'What do you mean?'

'Whether she accepts her fate with Sudipto or takes her chances with Nilanjan, neither option is safe, fool-proof, or easy. In both the alternatives, she will need to leave home and begin a new life elsewhere.'

He was quiet, thoughtful.

'How tough has it been for you, Disha? Leaving everything familiar behind and beginning anew?'

Can a man ever really know?

'I think I am more used to it.'

'In what way?'

'I didn't have someone like you to always take care of me. I learnt to fight my battles since I was very young.'

'In that way, you were luckier. You weren't given a false sense of security only to be disillusioned later.' His tone was bitter. 'I just didn't read the signals right. If I had just toed Ma's line in everything and had not alienated her, perhaps she'd have been more amenable.'

'Everything, like what?'

'Like keeping a safe distance from you.'

I straightened and moved out of his embrace. Words failed me.

'And do you know why I haven't kept a safe distance?'

The sinking feeling at the pit of my stomach pre-empted any reply.

He started the car with a sigh. 'That place feels alien, it

no longer feels like home. But for Nina's sake, I've got to be there.'

⁂

His mother was pacing the verandah when we drove up. She gave me a dour look. 'Go up to your room. I need to talk to my son.'

Sid held my wrist to stop me and gave me the lightest of the three bags he was carrying. He hoisted the others comfortably on his shoulders and then walked indoors beside me. He continued to ignore his mother.

Aunty Parul and her three sons were out, attending a family friend's anniversary party. The table had the rest of the women of the house, and Sid, Joe, Dave and Jimmy. No one served at the table as the number was small. Nina barely ate. Sid answered the questions the boys asked him about the concert. There seemed to be tension in the room.

'I've never talked about these things before, Shubhra, but now I think I should have,' Aunty Karen began.

Only Joe engaged and it was more as a protest, 'Can't we all just enjoy lunch and go into whatever this is after?'

She refused to be steered away. From the way her eyes flitted to Sid, it was evident this was all for his benefit.

'Why do you think I rarely go downstairs and never set foot in the kitchen?' she answered herself.

'Those two saintly and pious women you see on the ground floor, they were very different with me, almost witches. I was tormented and abused, treated like a lowly outcaste for about fifteen years since I came to this house. I suffered it all in silence. For Amulya. And later, for the kids.'

'Ma, talk about other things, please,' Joe urged her.

'Joe, as a victim of that kind of discrimination for the colour of my skin and because of my faith, do you think I can ever run the risk of that happening again in Nina's life?'

'I'm sorry, Ma. But it is Nina's life,' Joe pointed out.

'As parents, we have experience and deeper knowledge of the ways of the world. And sometimes, we have to be concerned for the future of our children. I have done what I have for Nina's good.'

There was an awkward silence for a while. Now, she looked at Sid. 'You are the most precious, the most generous, and impractical of all my children. You are oversensitive and kind to a fault. When I see someone completely unsuitable and unworthy manipulating that goodness, I have to take a stand. I will intervene to do what is best for your future. As your mother, I have to do whatever it takes to protect your interests.'

Sid looked down at his plate. Shadows were flitting across his face.

'Who is exploiting Sid?' Dave asked, clearly in a fog.

Sid pushed his chair back and left the room before anybody could react. Aunty burst out in anger and sorrow. 'I simply can't understand what has got into him.'

⁂

Sid wasn't in his room. I tried the music room. On an acoustic guitar, he was picking at strings with an expression that revealed that his mind was elsewhere. My presence didn't seem to register as he bent close to his strings. I came and knelt by his chair. As always, his music was a shower of sound with the clarity of diamonds even when it was played this softly. He tinkered with the guitar for about ten minutes and then kept it away to rest against a wall. I switched on the tānpurā, and as the drone filled the room with the melody of all its notes, I spoke to him.

'This song is fairly slow. Do you think it would sound better at the concert if I tweaked the tempo?'

I didn't wait for him to reply but launched into my Madhuvanti rāg pradhān. He heard me in silence.

'The tempo doesn't matter. In fact, I think the song and the gāyaki lose out if it is rushed. The tarānā is upbeat. So there will be a good contrast in the two numbers you sing.'

'You know how we do a kind of sawāl-jawāb? I was wondering whether I could do it as fragments of tāns where I sing the notes at high speed. Only this time, I thought of using the ākār instead. Like this...'

I demonstrated about six short fragments.

'Sounds good. The drawback is that though there is movement or variation in notes, the beats are even throughout. The sawāl-jawāb works mainly if we can play around with the beat.'

It made me stop to reconsider. 'Maybe I'll have to make the tān strings comprise a series of miniscule fragments where the combinations and pauses provide the variations you want in the beat.'

'Do you think you can make that work?'

'I can try.'

I reached out and switched off the electronic tānpurā that had been playing faintly in the background. For a while, I sat absorbed in thoughts of notes and how to arrange them in tāns, to provide good layakāri. I thought of all the complex tihāi combinations I could generate. Absent-mindedly, I reached out for the bag I had brought along with me. It contained a bottle of water and two bars of chocolate from what Sid had given me in my kit that I had saved. I passed a bar to Sid while I took a small sip of water.

'I'm not hungry, Disha.'

'Nina needs you now. Please, Sid, don't do stupid things and let her down.'

'Did I tell you food is forbidden in this room?'

20

Helplessly Hoping

*I*ntimacy is strangely addictive. When somebody holds you close, that warmth becomes a haven. And you grow to seek its shelter. The proximity with Sid was such, the communication so beautiful that, despite all, I had simply changed my address to where he was.

The only antidote to this form of homelessness was that, mercifully, Sid wasn't ever too far away. We practised together though a lot less rigorously now as too much was happening around him. And in his interactions with me, there was still that unwavering closeness and the shared music that made all the difference to me.

One morning, Nina came to my room. Our interactions were usually sparse so I was surprised.

'Do you know where Sid is?'

'No, Nina, we have a practice session only tomorrow. Perhaps you could call.'

'It isn't that important. I was just wondering, that is all.'

She walked around the room, touching objects on the

shelves and tables, fixing and straightening them.

'Lila is coming down next week. For the wedding...' her voice trailed off. 'Can I ask you to do something for me, Disha? Would you talk to Sid?'

'About what, Nina?'

'Tell him I've made my peace with...with whatever happens next. It is not as if I was in love with Nilanjan or something. Or even if I was, I don't know if it meant anything at all, if that alone would have worked things out.'

She paused. 'Do you understand what I am saying?'

I nodded.

'I am going into this with an open mind now. Only, I am very worried about Sid.'

Her brow creased. I hadn't seen an unhappier young woman.

'No one loves Ma the way Sid does. Never before has he disagreed with her on anything. He actually worships her and she knows it too. This is the worst thing that could have happened—to either of them.'

'I am sure things will work out in time.'

It was a beautiful portrait, her standing at the window, among the sheer whites, with her blond hair flowing. Suddenly, she felt close—like a sister.

'Disha, do you remember that evening when Sid wanted to tell you about me?'

'I guess.' My answer was a little uncertain. I was unsure what it was she wanted me to recall.

'He had reminded me who you were. Did you ever

wonder what he meant by that?'

'I haven't given it a thought.'

I really hadn't. She moved. At the study table beside the window, she stood stacking the books carefully, sorting them out by size.

'It seems you are really young. How old are you?'

'I'll soon be twenty-one.'

She didn't reply but disrupted the stack of books to redo it, slowly.

❧

My introduction to the fabled Lila was abrupt. I was on my way back from the bathroom when I ran into a woman with Jayashree and she stopped to stare at me curiously.

'So, this is the orphan!'

'Hello, you must be Lila. My name is Disha.'

Her features were so similar to Sid's it was uncanny.

'You must give her the respect due. You should call her Lila Di,' Jayashree corrected me sharply.

Lila turned to her. 'She isn't even pretty. Why did you think so? I'd probably rate her as passable.'

'Hey, Lil! Sorry, I was out last night.' We were all standing outside Joe's room. He hugged her and then asked, 'So, what do I get from the mighty USA?'

'Your adorable older sister and endless babysitting duties. I hope you love both your gifts.'

Joe tugged at the towel I had wrapped around my head and it came loose. He caught it as it fell. The act was so strongly Sid.

'Did you meet Disha?'

'Yeah, and I was just telling Joy that she is at best passably attractive. I can't imagine what the fuss is all about.'

Joe did something strange—he held me close to him, almost protectively.

'Well your opinion doesn't matter. I happen to think Disha is gorgeous. Plus, she sings like an angel in mufti.'

Lila stared at me, quickly reassessing before commenting sourly.

'I didn't imagine you were the one to worry about.'

'It's not your worry in any case, Lil. Don't you have a life yet?'

'Of course I do. But I'm not going to sit back and watch weird things happen to the family.'

'The weirdest thing that ever happened to this family is you!' Joe rumbled, laughing heartily at his clever comeback.

֍

At lunch, Sid was directly addressed. 'I can't organize the wedding without you, Sid. It's impossible for me.'

Everyone turned silent. The strain was known to all. Sid answered, almost murmuring inside his glass of water. 'Good, then call it off.'

Lila bristled. It was apparent she was the bossiest offspring. 'Why do you have to give him so much importance? Tell me what needs to be done and I'll do it.'

'Will all of you just let Sid eat in peace?' Nina spoke up.

'What's stopping your precious Sid from eating?' Lila's

tone was belligerent.

In that taut atmosphere, the bull in a china shop that was Joe went on a spree. 'Less than twelve hours in the country and you are back with a bang, Lil. You sure spread sweetness and light wherever you go.'

'Shut up, Joe. You talk far too much these days.'

He grinned wider. Jousting with his gang of six had made him a boss in this milieu. 'You think I am Ateesh? That I'll jump to whatever you say because I am scared of your hissy fits?'

'Ateesh isn't scared of me.'

'Poor man! With you out of the way now, abolition of slavery or not, he must be taking his first few breaths as a free man back home in Denver.'

There was laughter and high-fives.

'Ma!' Lila turned to Aunty Karen for support.

Aunty Parul responded, reaching out to slap Joe hard on his shoulder. 'Don't talk rubbish all the time.'

'Ouch!' He rubbed his shoulder blade, wincing. 'Now I know why Uncle is the strong silent types.'

'If that's all it takes to keep you silent, I'm willing to oblige.'

Lila looked around the table. Her eyes rested on Sid. 'So you still lead your wasteful useless life, bumming around with your guitar and your worthless musician pals. And...' She turned around to look at the group of six in full attendance today, all still scruffy in the track pants or shorts they'd slept in. 'And only Tony is in office.'

'Tony has to be, Lil,' Jimmy informed her.

'Why?'

'That is his only refuge from our dear Jayashree.'

More laughter and high-fives followed. Jayashree's face puckered up in irritation. 'Tony loves his work.'

'If I were him, I'd love my secy too.'

'Tony's secy? Ewww! She must be forty-five.'

'Still, heaven. If the alternative is our dear friend, Joy.'

'Ma!' Jayashree's voice was shrill. 'Why aren't you saying anything?'

But Aunty Karen was only looking at Sid, sorrow etched on her face.

⁂

Those days, the household was chaotic and high-pitched. Sid did help his dad with the organizing though he still refused to have anything to do with his mother. From the fringes of all that activity, I observed how Sid handled the pressure, organized and cool-headed, while Tony would snap at the smallest request or keep pointing out flaws in what was proposed. At every dinner, Sid would calmly update the others, list out all that remained to be done. The rest of the guys simply looked stricken when even the smallest chore was apportioned to them.

The frenetic activity against the backdrop of tension in the household often resulted in extreme unease. It also meant that no one really had much time to notice my presence. And, in a way, I receded into the backdrop, not venturing

Helplessly Hoping

out much and keeping as much to myself as I could. I barely saw Sid at all.

During a practice session, Vidyut played back recordings from both our performances. The guys did this during the breaks, analysing elements in great detail and discussing ways to further innovate. I heard my parts with care. Even to my unaccustomed ear, there was a marked change in my voice quality from the first concert to the second for which there was no explanation—except for the fact that I had grown immensely as a person in that time span. I wondered how I could keep that growth intact, how by the time of our Kharagpur appearance, I could live up to the standards of the band.

And soon enough, in the midst of all the chaos of the preparations for the wedding, the Kharagpur concert crept up on us.

21

Rock You Like a Hurricane

When Nishith asked Ashraf for the keys to his bike, he dug it out of the pocket of his jeans and tossed it.

'Disha, come for a ride with me.'

Ashraf turned to me. 'Performance is just over an hour away.'

I heard the sober note of caution in his voice and felt the need to allay his doubts.

'Besides, I'm terrified of bikes,' I looked at Nishith as I said it.

'You are terrified of life, Disha. Come along and taste some.'

'Am not.'

'Alright then, come for a walk with me.'

'There are six thousand people less than 400 metres away. The place is jam-packed. There is a rock show going on. Walk where?'

'I need to talk to you.'

I got up rather reluctantly.

'She has a performance coming up. Remember that,' Ashraf cautioned.

Nishith pretended not to hear him. He found the stairs to the terrace above the set of rooms we were occupying as a green room. Half a field away was a vast open-air auditorium and faint sounds of the ongoing concert wafted out to us despite all the speakers being turned the other way.

'What did you mean, Disha, that I was being molested back then?'

'This isn't the time or place for that discussion.'

As if my remark had gone deeper than intended, he looked more doubtful and vulnerable than I had seen him.

'Whenever two people come together, there is always a chance that one partner has more experience while the other has less or none.'

I refused to answer, not quite happy with this conversation, more specifically, its timing.

'Or is it that you felt as the man, I should have been the more experienced one?'

'I didn't give it too much thought. Shall we go down?'

'Let me redeem myself in your eyes. Will you let me introduce you to who you are inside, what you can feel and experience if you trust another with your desires?'

I turned to walk away and he gripped my wrist with strength I hadn't expected of him. And he pulled me close, till I was just a fraction of an inch away.

'You've known me for a while now, Disha. Don't you feel anything at all for me? Won't you reciprocate this burning desire I have for you?'

I couldn't bring myself to look at him. I knew exactly what he meant.

'A woman wants a man just as badly as he wants her.'

His palm guided mine as he made me feel the skin on his stomach, his chest, his shoulders and back again in small intimate circles under his T-shirt. I slowly freed my hand and walked to the end of the terrace, blank and frightened. He joined me there slowly.

'The guys all speculate what Sid feels for you. No one talks about what you feel for Sid. It makes me terribly envious, Disha. Except, you should know that every woman Sid knows looks at him with those same eyes.'

'Why are we talking about Sid?'

'It is because of him that you refuse to acknowledge that you love me too.'

'When did you not know I love you, Nishith? I have the moral fibre to accept what I feel.'

'And?'

I turned away. The evening spread like a replica of our own abstruseness.

'If you begin to cry, I am not sure Ashraf will not kill me.'

He held me now, very gently. His voice was the coarsest I had ever heard it be.

'I would never have tolerated sharing the mike as the vocalist of Derozio Dreams with anyone but you.'

'I know.'

'I don't want to marry you or anything.'

'I know that too.'

'But I do love you a lot.'

'I do, too. Heck, forget about marrying you, I wouldn't even kiss you.'

'That hurts. Not even one on the cheek?'

'Idiot!' I leaned and kissed his cheek. Under all that he was a fabulous person whose presence I had not been untouched by.

'You are a very special human being, Nishith.'

'I know. But you can keep telling me that.'

We stood together in happy intimate silence.

'Why don't you have girlfriends, Nishith?'

'Because I tell every girl I like at the outset that I don't want to marry them.'

'So is it the girl or the idea of matrimony?'

'In most cases, it is both. In your case, it is just matrimony.'

I laughed. 'You flatter almost as good as you sing.'

His eyes turned serious. 'You know what, Disha? I sing a lot better when you are around. It's crazy, but it's true.'

Nishith took me to the back, near the door of the room. 'I feel a little antsy now. I'll just go and check out our competition. It's a band called Aural. I've only heard them once before, and back then, they were really sucky.'

I paused to take a deep breath before pushing open the door. We had managed to keep it light but it had been no less frazzling. I felt like I'd been scooped out from within. By the look Ashraf threw at me, I realized he'd been a little anxious. I mustered a faint smile with some effort. As I went to sit beside him, I discovered he had his own demons too.

'I'm not gay, no matter what Nishith says.'

'I know Nishith well enough by now to know he will say anything.'

'Not that I have anything against homosexual people. I know how it feels to be marginalized.'

'How have you been marginalized?'

'Surely you know about my faith and the scenario worldwide post 9/11.'

'The outlook seems bleak or bright depending on your circumstances, even your geographical location.'

'And in India we are a minority, a suspect minority.'

'You are an artist, a musician. You play Western classical and Western current music that owes it genesis to church music, hymns, choirs and the need to go beyond them. You live in India and you have been influenced by Indian classical traditions, part of which are also rooted in temples and prayers. You have the dervishes and the entire Sufi tradition of transcendental mysticism. You can identify with all of this. The only god here is beauty and creation. Art and music are by essence secular.'

'In what way? How has it been secular for you?'

'My village, it's called Hamirpur, and we suspect the name comes from the rāg. The population there is exactly fifty-fifty; there are no minorities there. My Guruji was Ustad Wahid Khan Saheb and all the best bhajans I know, I've learnt from him. And he sang them with equal fervour as he sang qawwālis and other Sufiāna kalām. There was a point where my voice was faltering from all the strain and he advised me to begin each practice session with about fifteen minutes of just singing "aum". And when he sang to demonstrate... What a meaningful and profound sound it was!'

'You miss your village terribly, don't you?'

'Why would you say that?'

'Your eyes were so happy as you spoke.'

And immediately, I was dragged back to my life in Kolkata, my struggles to maintain my dignity, my altered circumstances and how hard I needed to try to make peace with what my life now was. But the worst of it all was accepting how just my presence seemed to have caused complications.

Ashraf seemed mortified. 'I was worried Nishith would make you cry and look what I've done.'

'It's not you, Ashraf. You, every member of the band, the music...all of you are the only positives I have in my life now.'

He just stared at my tears in horror.

The crowd roiled and boiled over at Nishith's greeting. 'It's been a long wild night, Kharagpur. Let's make it wilderrrrr!'

His voice was drowned out in the screams of assent. 'Guys, we are an obscure band from Kolkata and we call ourselves Derozio Dreams!'

There were some protests.

He engaged in a conversation with a bunch of guys in the front row. 'What did you say? Not obscure?'

'Nooooo!!' went the crowd.

'Wow! That means you guys do stuff other than your Fourier transforms and relative grading manoeuvres. And after tonight, I hope all of you listen to a lot more of a religion we pursue called "rock".'

The crowd listened intently. Nishith had that power. 'And now I'd like to introduce you to some of its acolytes. On the drums, Vidyut!'

Vidyut's sticks went flailing into a crazy roll after which he tore into a frenzied eight by six, and in a minute, Shady joined him to duel momentarily on the beat.

'The boss of bass—Shady! And now with lightning fingers, on keyboards, my brother Ashraf!'

Ashraf joined in, the trio skimming on the edgy mathematics of time as beats for a brief while.

'It is no great secret that Derozio Dreams is synonymous with the phenom, Sid!'

There was a loud roar. Everyone stopped playing. Sid's riff erupted in the silence—crackling, intense, intimate and powerful. Nishith came up to where I stood with a naughty smile, aware that the spotlights had followed him.

'She's reticent and shy. She's inimitable. And she's what Derozio Dreams had been praying for—Disha.'

Still smiling, he hugged me amid a medley of wolf whistles and then walked to the middle of the stage, grinning. 'Isn't love a wonderful thing?'

The crowd, gender-wise lopsided as these places are, understood him and agreed.

'And just to keep this feeling of romance alive and to celebrate that we are young and carefree, we give you our classic romantic song—Cirrhosis.'

In reality, that number was hard rock bordering on metal, an ode to alcohol as the only cure to women. There was a pause of silence as the audience grappled with Nishith's joke, and then with a jangle of potent sounds, the concert took off.

The final scream of the song saw Nishith fall back on the stage. The crowd lapped it up. Still lying down, he announced the next offering. It amazed me that he could sustain his antics, his voice and his warm engaged chats with the crowd seamlessly for three hours or more.

'So, guys, I am told you barely get to hear a female voice out here. The ratio is that terribly skewed!'

The crowd responded with the groans of a raw nerve touched and Nishith continued his conversation with the crowd. Into the mike, he said, 'Yeah, dude, that's the problem with the world today—not enough women, not the real nice ones anyway. And so, here's one voice that will stay with you for the rest of the year, if not the rest of your lives.'

I entered the stage area as Vidyut tapped out successive phrases on the drums, which I mirrored with phrases from my taranā. And then, all stilled, I launched a cappella into the first line of the composition. On the cross the band swung in, full strength, and it sounded magical in the night.

When Nishith needed to come in, he stood beside me, his arm holding me close, and our moment from the terrace dissolved.

22

Rock and Roll Ain't Noise Pollution

The crowd was knowledgeable about music, especially Dreams' music, and there were requests to play quite a few originals that only diehard fans would know of. There was sizzling energy and the music kept it alive with inputs from Nishith. I marvelled again at what a brilliant frontman he was. We ended up being close to three hours in concert.

An organizer then took the mike. 'May I please request the band to remain onstage?'

This was post the last encore performance, after we had all stepped forward on the stage to take our bows and had dispersed again to dismantle our equipment.

'This year we had decided to begin a new system at the institute in the invitations to professional bands. We had downloaded seven-minute clips from eight contenders and asked everyone here to vote for the top pro band they wanted to see in concert at our annual youth fest. And winning by a resounding margin of almost a thousand votes out of a possible four thousand and three hundred, it's Derozio Dreams!'

Someone came onstage with a plaque. 'And to present a small token of our appreciation we invite Professor Gaurang Mukhopadhyay, the Dean of Cultural Affairs, to hand Derozio Dreams their memento.'

Vidyut and Nishith stepped onstage to take the plaque from the smiling professor, who was dressed in formal clothes, looking patently out of place amid the swarms of black T-shirts, invariably festooned with skulls.

The dean took the mike. 'I haven't attended a rock show in over twenty years now. And I came in tonight with my children with a sense of trepidation. It was a pleasant surprise and I must declare that I've had a very enjoyable evening. It is all thanks to the versatility of the music played by Derozio Dreams.' He smiled. 'Of course, I must confess I liked the fusion elements sung by Disha the best. I understand Hindustani classical music better than...'

But he was drowned out by shouts from the crowd—all of them seemed to be telling him that he wasn't expected to eye girls at his age.

'It's a new twist to cultural "affairs", Gaurango!' a heckler's voice floated over the hubbub.

The dean responded with a long-suffering sporting smile as he continued, '...better than rock. I guess it hasn't passed my students' notice that in addition to being a brilliant singer, Disha is an attractive young lady as well.'

There were screams of near ecstasy now. 'But that doesn't

take away from the excellent performances of Vidyut, Ashraf, Shailesh, Sid and Nishith.'

He mentioned the names without consulting a paper and I knew then that he was an intelligent man, an unlikely fan who had really felt the music that evening. There was a massive applause. Not a single individual had left the audience yet, though everyone knew the music was done for the night.

'I would earnestly request the band to make their music available in CD format for fans and for neo-converts like me.' He turned to Nishith.

'Yes, sir. We are planning to release a CD soon. Maybe in about three months' time.'

The crowd supported the idea heartily.

Now, Nishith spoke. 'This is a huge honour for us, guys. Only one thing makes it all worthwhile. And that's the love and support we get from our fans who appreciate what we do.'

He turned to look at Sid in the wings, 'And it couldn't have been done without my brothers, each member of Derozio Dreams, who have been to me more than family.'

Everyone cheered again and then a collective voice called out, 'Sid! Sid!'

'Come, Ashraf, Shady.'

And he held me by the elbow and took me along too. All six of us stood lined up. The dean now handed over the memento to Nishith and Vidyut and shook hands with all of us.

'You guys rock!' a lone voice called out in the night. And then, the same voice added, 'Say something, Sid.'

It became a more insistent chorus until Sid took the mike. 'I prefer to let my guitar say it all. It's been awesome to come and play for you guys. May we keep meeting whenever we can. And may music light our lives forever.'

How he stood, the words he found and the simplicity with which he spoke was quintessentially Sid and caused a mad wave of uncontrollable love surge through me. As the dean left the stage, Nishith found Sid to give him the plaque and hugged him hard. All the guys hugged each other. In the end, Nishith held me, his face buried in the crook of my neck. My arms slowly came around to hold him too, learning the new language of rockers.

'You were amazing tonight.'

Again, I tried to stay out of everyone's way. A bunch of student organizers came up on stage, some to help, others to talk to the band.

'You seem awfully young to be in a rock band, Disha,' a young man told me.

I tried to smile, but strangers behaving as if they had known me all my life really made me wary. A long silence followed, which was awkward for both of us.

'So you live in Kolkata. And do you give solo classical performances too?'

'No, I belong to the band.'

Perhaps Nishith saw me struggling and came over to join us. 'Are you hungry, Disha? I'm famished.'

'We have a canteen that is open till three in the morning. We could get you what you want.'

'Let's get Ashraf's bike and go, Disha.'

'I'm not hungry at all. I'm dead exhausted.'

It was close to one by now.

'I could drop you to your quarters if you like,' the student offered.

But Sid wouldn't have it. 'Hold on for five minutes. I'll take you back.'

In the car, Sid commented. 'I barely saw you all evening. You disappeared after your soundcheck.'

'You were otherwise occupied, Sid.'

'What does that mean?'

I looked out ahead.

'You know I keep my distance from you in the presence of the guys. Always have.'

'If your life is much simpler in every way if you just keep your distance from me, why do you bother with me? Why am I in your life at all? Or am I in it, Sid?'

'What do you think?'

'I don't think about these things. I have no wish to lose my mind.'

He found my palm and raised it to his face, scraping against its back with his chin.

'Why would thinking about me make you lose your mind?'

'What have you been smoking today?'

'Nothing. Why?'

'You usually need to be drunk or doped out of your mind to want to be with me.'

I had no business being this aggressive with him or needlessly quarrelsome. I blame my internal misery.

'Do you want an account of every moment I have spent with you? I recall each nanosecond, every moment I've experienced with greater honesty and clarity than all your sobriety could have given you.'

'That may be. But I'm sure your mind was so fogged you wouldn't have even known which woman out of your hordes you were with.'

Sid let my hand go. There was silence as the car pulled up at the gates of a faculty bungalow that had been vacant and had been allotted to the band for the night. He let us in with his keys. He stood, barely inside, waiting for me to go to my room that was just as bare as the others were but for the white-sheeted single mattress on the floor. Something drew me back to him. I closed the door.

'Will you kiss me, Sid? I need to know that you would even if you weren't intoxicated.'

I felt gentle fingers stroke my face.

'You sounded perfect tonight, Disha. As if you had practised each nuance a thousand times in this past month. Are you upset with me for not being there, inaccessible for far too long now?'

I shook my head, unable to look away from the darkening pupils of his eyes.

'I'm going through a very rough patch in my life. Nothing seems sane or under control any more. I...I need your understanding, Disha.'

He bent to kiss me on my forehead and continued kissing my face in irregular showers—the kisses far more sensual than any other touch.

'What made you practise so hard?'

His lips were close to mine. I turned to them as I spoke. 'I wanted to justify my place in the band.'

'You did tonight, far sooner than I had expected you to become a polished pro.'

Our lips touched now, only tentatively. I closed my eyes in anticipation. And I felt Sid's breath rise and fall heavier now. I felt his body draw closer—hungry, aflame. Something that seemed like an undeniable disquiet need seemed to explode between us. It seemed to engulf us in its power.

He stopped and pulled away to look at me. My hand touched his back, initially nervous. In a while, I began exploring him, knowing more of him. I moved away to make a little space between his body and mine as I touched his hard stomach, his chest and his shoulders. And in that moment, I knew Nishith had been right. There are times a woman wants a man just as much.

23

Bohemian Rhapsody

There was a barely perceptible creak as my door was pushed open. I sat up in the dark. Sid stood against the door he had just locked behind him.

'I haven't touched a drop of drink.'

'That's unlike you, Sid.'

I lay back slowly in the dark. Sid didn't move from his place near the door.

'Disha, it bothers me that you are just twenty. Tell me I am not making a mistake.'

'I can't get you printed invitation cards at this point.'

He moved slowly to the mattress, and stood there, trying to see me in the dark.

'You surprise me all the time.'

My hand touched his knee as he sat on the floor.

'Every person in the audience loved you tonight. Do you know that?'

'They don't know me at all.'

'I do.'

'What do you know about me?'

'Will you let me show you?'

He let me pull him closer to me. I moved to lay my head on his shoulder.

'I know that you have tens of thousands of screaming fans, hundreds of interested girls, a houseful of a very loving family, and yet inside you are lonely. Like you are an orphan too. Like me.'

His fingers came up to stroke my arm.

'And you drown yourself in the music and the practice. But after every concert you need to confront yourself all over again.'

'What would you recommend?'

'This. Even if it is trivial and ephemeral. This is all I have, all I can really give you.'

I hoped that he would respond, say something. He didn't. He continued to stroke my arm—his touch somehow drained out my exhaustion, making me fully awake. I nestled in deeper, my head finding a more comfortable spot on his shoulder. I turned to hold him lightly, and my palm rested against his chest. I drew away immediately, guiltily. I had touched him more intimately than I had intended to.

Then I reminded myself that the theme of the night was intimacy and beyond, and I had to virtually train my palm to touch him again, hoping he wouldn't realize that my fingers were shaking. There was a slow progression from inhibition to exploration and beyond, to pleasure and desire. At one point, I stopped and curled my fingers back, bringing my hands to my sides.

'What happened?'

I shook my head. I felt him pull me up; both of us were hesitant, our lips restrained and cautious rather than passionate. And even then, it felt powerful.

I voiced a doubt. 'Sid, do you know how this works?'

'Let's sleep. It's been a really long day.'

Was this rejection? Was he telling me something? Why was I feeling both relief and disappointment?

Sid now rearranged the pillows and settled in. He reached out to hold me close but lightly and I prayed for sleep.

Something woke me up. I couldn't tell what it was. Perhaps it was some sound and I waited for it to recur. I knew he was awake too.

'Kiss me, Sid.'

He didn't answer but his arms gathered me in fiercely. And he kissed me—this kiss had the passion and the recklessness of desire. Now, Sid touched me as I had and it constricted my breathing. My body needed his and as I tried to control my breathing, I hoped he knew how I felt.

I realized much later that Sid taught me lovemaking in the same way he taught me music and all the lessons in life—with love, patience, restraint and generosity. He would stop to talk to me, ask me questions that distracted me from what was happening. He seemed to understand my fears and needs, and his wish to allay both was clear. He taught me how to be a part of him, to complement him and to fill that loneliness with love just as I had set out to.

There came a time when I lay there, scarcely breathing, all my senses so heightened that a faint touch seemed to pierce and touch me deep within, almost at the core of my soul. Sid pushed back the hair from my face, his fingers wispy, and feather light, and I sensed the holding back, the mild withdrawal.

My mouth was against his, inviting him to return.

'What is it, Sid?'

His fingers were heavier against my face.

'Now it involves hurting you, Disha. And I can't do it.'

'It hurts anyway.'

'What hurts?'

'What I am feeling inside. Like I am in a tunnel and there's no respite, no turning back until I see this through.'

'Are you sure there's no turning back?'

I kissed him now, rough and ragged. My body reached out to him, hoping he would know what my words would fail to tell him.

༄

As we set off, I looked at the buildings.

'Something about this place reminds me of Kalimpong.'

Sid turned to me, 'Why Kalimpong?'

'I was a boarder there for seven years. I think the campus reminded me of that.'

'I didn't know you went to boarding school.'

'Baba was so busy initially with the setting up of all those cooperatives that he couldn't take care of us. We were sent away. I came back for my graduation though, at a local college.'

'Did you do alright at the boarding school? Didn't you miss your family?'

'I had been close only to Ma in those days and Ma was dead.'

His hand reached out to take mine. I needed the comfort of his touch.

'I was okay, I guess.'

'Did you do anything after college?'

'I thought you knew. I used to be Baba's executive assistant. I worked alongside him, even through college, almost fourteen hours each day. And when I lost him... I could do all the work he'd taught me, Sid. But no one would let me because I am a woman and so young. They wouldn't even let me stay on in my own house. And today, I need to take refuge in Amulya Uncle's.'

I let out a sigh. 'It's all done and gone. I have to make peace with my reality now.'

Vidyut had committed to giving a couple of guys from Aural a lift back to Kolkata, so Nishith decided to come in our car. He chose to be uncommunicative while Sid and I chatted, and he sat slouched in the back seat, staring at the passing vistas.

'Is there water here?'

I turned to Nishith. 'There's a bottle in the pocket of that green rucksack. Please pass that on, Nishith.'

He did. Sid slowed down to drink.

'Why are you this thirsty? We'll need to stop and get more water too.'

'Stopping is a good idea. Let's have gallons of tea. I'm terribly sleepy.'

'And why are you sleepy, Sid?'

He gave me a burning look. I felt it singe my insides. I tried to keep it light. 'You shouldn't be putting Nishith's and my life at risk, driving half-asleep.'

Nishith spoke in a drawl, 'After last night I don't mind dying, Disha.'

No one in the car was unaware what he was referring to. Sid nonchalantly ruffled the top of my head. 'And my life is expendable, is it?'

I looked at him, unable to comprehend what he was telling me.

'Let's stop for that tea.'

❦

We returned home to the realization that only five days remained for Nina's wedding. Relatives had begun to move in. Others who couldn't leave their homes in Kolkata came in early in the morning and stayed on till as late as their schedules for the day permitted. The house seemed to be bursting at its seams and the noise unbearable even in a household that had withstood the onslaught of the formidable six.

I found solace in small things. Lila's two little kids, Arun and Maya, baffled by the chaos, often retreated to my room and I spent a lot of my time with them. They took to coming to me with their requests for snacks and what they'd like at mealtimes and I tried to rustle up whatever I could from their list of requests—burgers, sandwiches, shakes and fries.

Aunty Karen noticed this. 'There is so much good food around. Why are they always being given bread at mealtimes?'

'Let them be, Ma,' Lila defended me. 'Disha is really only helping. They are not used to this kind of food.'

'Then when will they learn?'

Arun turned to his grandmother with earnest eyes. 'These are really good. Disha makes them just as we like them.'

Meanwhile, Sid was engulfed in all that needed to be done. He normally left the house even before any of us woke up. We only saw him sometimes at dinner. He had just speared a piece of meat from my plate when Aunty Karen snapped. 'If you need more food, just serve yourself some or ask me. Don't eat out of other people's plates.'

Now, Joe found himself another piece and popped it into his mouth with a grin.

'You won't understand, Ma. It's more fun this way.'

Their father's tone was indulgent. 'It may be fun for you two, but Disha needs to eat as well.'

'No, Dad. Disha has practically no exercise and she's getting fat.' Sid turned to me with a wicked smile. 'Joe and I are doing her a favour.'

'She isn't fat. In fact, I think she's lost so much weight since she's come to stay,' Aunty Parul remarked, serving me some more of the stew. 'I think, Sid, you are making her overwork.'

'Right now, I think Arun and Maya are.'

'Don't say that, Sid,' Lila snapped. 'It's a huge burden off me. They even let her bathe them and put them to bed. Otherwise I could never have shopped and prepared the invites and all the stuff I need to.'

⁂

A pattern slowly established itself as Sid began to call each evening. He had nothing specific to say. He would just ask me questions about my day, what I'd had for lunch, and what the kids were up to. It wasn't what we talked about, but what we didn't that stayed with me long after the call was disconnected. It just felt nice to hear his voice sounding light and momentarily unburdened.

We were leaving the room after breakfast on a rare occasion that Sid was around, the day before the wedding. At the door, I came up against Nana, Aunty Karen's mother. She was a dignified woman with a straight back and a beautiful smile. She took my hand and turned to her daughter. We were holding up all the people behind us—the uncles, Sid and other guests in the crowd.

'Who is this girl, Karen? You haven't introduced us?'

Aunty flushed. 'She's Disha. She's...err...she has come to stay with us.'

'Such a lovely girl!'

24
Free Fallin'

For Nina's wedding, I wore what I had worn to Deepa's. It was a pale-green silk with a broad gold border, teamed with a brocade blouse. Danny took Lila, the kids and me in a car to the venue at a private club. And all of us were swallowed in the crowd and the simultaneous little dramas that play out in charged gatherings.

Lila turned to me. 'I'm leaving the kids to you entirely. I'll be just too busy to keep an eye on them.'

Danny who stood near me as she turned away to execute her grand entrance wasn't too happy. 'They are her kids. And you need to enjoy the wedding too.'

'It's her sister's wedding. She will be very busy.'

'Lil? Not a chance.'

I recall at Deepa and Deena's weddings, Baba and I had virtually no time to breathe. Here, everything seemed to have been outsourced to organizers and the family was mostly free to socialize with their large number of guests and to enjoy the event.

Each frame of the wedding played out almost by itself. The groom's motorcade arrived and the ceremonies began fairly early in the evening. An army of waiters served drinks and snacks, criss-crossing the lawns in smart uniforms. There was faint shehnai music in the background and it was accompanied by the gentle buzz of people talking in small groups.

I stayed on the fringes of the lawn with the kids. They were quiet, daunted by the number of strangers and the newness, and I joined them in remaining removed from it all. But I did observe the crowds, watching graceful women in elegant sarees and grave men adding colour and solemnity to the occasion. The kids wanted to eat something and we set off for the buffet tables across the well-lit lawns.

As we crossed a group of women, Lila turned. 'Have they eaten?'

'We weren't hungry, Mommy. We are going now.'

Aunty Karen was there too, talking to a knot of well-dressed women, their silks lustrous against the deep green of the lawns.

'These are my grandchildren—Arun and Maya.'

The kids each clung to my hands. Now Aunty turned to a beautiful young woman in shimmering white who stood beside her.

'And have I introduced Monica?'

Her eyes trapped mine as she looked at me with significant hauteur before turning to her friends with a smile. 'Monica is Sid's girlfriend. I think I'll have another wedding to organize very soon.'

'Shall we get dinner?' I bent down to ask the kids and both of them nodded.

I helped them pick what they would eat and found us chairs away from the crowd. As the kids kept up a steady commentary on all the food they tasted, I was left alone with my searing thoughts. So, Sid was marrying soon! The pain of this was excruciating. Somehow, despite the women, the indirect warnings from everybody, I had gone and made such a complete ass of myself.

There had seemed something very deep and honest about Sid throughout that I had mistaken for reality, for strong integrity. Perhaps, that integrity mattered in his dealings with everybody except women, because he was probably weary of all women by now. What I had thought was so unique and precious between us had its mundane side too— of convenience and access. Of me being asinine enough to believe in fairy tales. It was idiotic of me to have imagined he would feel the same, be swept away as I had been on my first foray into the world of grown-up games. I sat steeped in regrets and bitter realizations now.

The object of my tumultuous thoughts was crossing the lawn. I longed to run to him with my problem, which was dumb because he was the problem. That night, he wore a kurta-pyjama in pure white cotton and he looked so unlike how I had ever seen him. As I tried not to feel that acrid threat of tears, I realized I knew him too little. Actually, he was almost a stranger, except that I had misinterpreted the basis of our proximity. I saw a tall figure in shimmering white approach him. He stopped and there was an inviting tilt to his head as he spoke. Then, she tucked her arm in his and led him away. Their heights were perfectly coordinated and they looked striking together. His choice of a bride was as impeccable as everything else that he did.

※

Sid found me much later. 'There you are. I have been looking all over for you. Let's go get dinner.'

I could not bring myself to look at him. He looked at me enquiringly.

'I'm sorry. I already ate.'

'Without me? Has something happened?'

I looked away hoping I wouldn't begin to cry.

'Come anyway. Just give me company.'

'I'm taking care of the kids.'

He stood there in silence. But Al came to find him. 'Uncle needs you, Sid. He wanted you to see him asap.'

Sid hesitated just for a moment more before turning to go.

'Why did you tell Uncle Sid you had eaten when you haven't, Disha?' Arun asked me solemnly.

※

We went home in small batches. Lila hadn't arrived yet and the kids came with me to sleep in my bed. It took some time to settle them into their room as Lila insisted. When I came back to my room, I still felt hollow and sleepless. I sat on my bed in the dark, distraught.

In the past, I had let Baba take over my life completely, dedicating every moment of my life to him, letting him drag me into a career that suited him because he needed that facilitation from me. When he left me, I had been left with nothing, left completely adrift. And I hadn't learnt my lesson. I had let Sid do the same with me. And now, when he would go, I would be devastated—orphaned once again.

After a long struggle with my thoughts, I felt a strong urge to go to the sit-out outside my door to breathe. The cold night air oddly did not sting as I stood there broken, seeking salve for my soul. I didn't hear Sid come and stand beside me. His look was alert, serious. I froze. His fingers gripped the railing just as mine did and his little finger reached out to stroke mine.

'You look very beautiful this evening, Disha.'

I snatched my hand away, and turning, fled to the refuge of my room.

25

Here I Go Again

Though the wedding itself had been seamlessly organized, there was complete chaos the day after. Numerous small ceremonies demanded knowledge of procedures that no one seemed to possess. There were requirements of specific offerings, and people were sent all over to procure them—it was as messy as it could get.

Lunch was hopelessly delayed. There were too many people and not enough chairs. I saw Sid working hard, trying to manage everything. Mats were spread on the first-floor dining-hall corridor and the younger folk were seated there.

In the midst of all this, Nina seemed untouched—serene and beautiful. Sudipto was nice, trying to cope with the strangeness of all these experiences. He seemed exhausted though. Careful observation found subtle stiffness between him and his bride but that was to be expected in any arranged marriage. Then, the household crowded into the large ground-floor verandah to see Nina off. She was remarkably calm. She stopped and spoke a word or two to everyone. She saw me at the edge of the crowd and came to me.

'Take care. Of him, too.'

She went on, only conspicuously ignoring her mother. The last person she spoke to was a copiously weeping Amulya Uncle. And then, she went down the steps with poise and found her seat in the car. Sudipto went around to the other side and the car shot out into the evening, into a new life for Nina. By now, everyone was weeping. I looked at Aunty Karen; she was pale and seemed upset. Nana came up beside me, her face crumpling from the sorrow of a granddaughter leaving home.

'Young lady, can you fix me a cup of tea? I feel exhausted.'

I led her to a seat in a smaller sitting room on the ground floor and switched on a fan for her.

'I'll be right back.'

I got Nana's tea and biscuits, and hot chocolate for the kids on a tray. When they were all done, I went back to my room. I took one step inside and stopped. Sid was sitting on my bed. I hadn't seen him on the verandah. He was miserable as he looked up at me, his face now ravaged with pain. I turned to bolt the door behind me.

'I've seen Nina every day of my life in the past twenty-four years.'

I walked towards him.

'Will he take care of her?'

I stopped in front of him. His words wobbled.

'What do you think, Disha? Will he?'

I reached out a palm to touch Sid's face. He grabbed me

now, holding me so hard it hurt, his face buried into me. My fingers touched his hair. 'She's a very balanced young lady, Sid. She'll be fine anywhere.'

Sid's grip around me tightened. I stroked his hair.

'Will you put me to sleep? I've not slept all of last night.'

He let me go and I went to draw the heavy white curtains across the window. The room was deliciously dark now. I came to the bed from the other side. Sid lay down close to me, his face hidden in my neck and shoulder. I tucked a hand under him to draw him closer to me. I felt his tears trickle down my neck and I soothed his shoulder and hair, kissing that inch of his forehead.

Sid seemed beyond recall as he wept, marooned in his grief. He probably didn't know I was with him. He certainly didn't know what a wreckage he had left behind inside me. It had been easy to resolve to distance myself from a smiling Sid, but when he was vulnerable I couldn't even for the sake of my sanity. As I lay there, caressing him, I cried too, at my situation and my despair. After a long while, Sid fell asleep, his ragged breathing turning even and peaceful.

I left a sleeping Sid and went down to dinner, afraid that my absence would bring someone to my room to investigate. Earlier, I had not been conscious of the time I spent in Sid's company. But now that he was going to marry Monica, I had to be more careful. I needn't have bothered. Only Nana, Lila and Joe were there and we had a silent abbreviated meal. When I got back to my room, Sid was gone.

Sid refused to attend Nina's reception. At lunch, everyone tried to convince him but he remained adamant.

'I have done all I could have for this wedding. I refuse to do any more.'

'Your absence will be noticed, Sid,' his father reasoned. 'Everyone knows the bride has three brothers. They would want to see you.'

'There will be seven brothers there. My absence will hardly matter.'

I rarely spoke at mealtimes as a rule. But this time, I had to. 'Think of Nina, Sid. She would like to see you.'

He turned to answer me, fairly patient. 'Nina knows she just needs to call me once for me to see her anytime. I refuse to be part of this tamasha—this massive homage to one unreasonable woman's ego—any more.'

For some reason, Joe didn't leave my side all evening and the kids and I were firmly enmeshed in the gang of six. They manhandled the kids who seemed to love the boisterous play and being tossed around. I just hoped they wouldn't notice my state and start off something, but they were better behaved at the groom's place and the evening unfolded without mishap.

That evening, too, we got home pretty late. I was in the car with Joe, Dave and the kids. In the silence of the drive, I realized how preoccupied my mind had been with Sid all evening. Some sort of resolution formed itself. I couldn't forsake Sid. I'd be with him as much as he needed me, for as long as he did. When he finally had others to cater to him,

I'd step back. Not because it was the sensible or giving thing to do. But I needed to do this for myself. I needed to know I had been there for Sid as thoroughly as he had for me.

Sid switched on the dim light of the room.

'When did you get back? Is anything the matter?'

'No. I...I was hoping you'd let me stay here tonight.'

He reached out to switch off the light. I moved to sit on the bed beside him. Our fingers intertwined.

'Are you alright, Sid?' I reached out, smoothing the front of his tee. 'Or did you have a really bad evening?'

'The house feels strange with no one in it. And why are you sounding so sad, Disha?'

'Am I? It's nothing.'

With ease, he lay his head on my lap as I sat, his arms wrapped loosely around my waist. I stared down at his back, the easy togetherness of the moment filling me with a sense of bleakness. What we did that night was a transgression in too many ways. From never having been out with a man in my Hamirpur days to practically begging to be made love to was a long hard transit. My naked body was offered as solace and I hoped that it was how Sid took it when his hard hungry mouth drank at my nipples.

26
Every Rose Has Its Thorn

Shailesh came to call me.

'Karen Madam wants to see you. She is in the ground-floor formal drawing room.'

These were unprecedented summons. There were many people in the room. From the family there was only Aunty Karen and she smiled graciously at me as I hesitated in the doorway.

'I guess you have seen Monica at Nina's marriage ceremony.'

She held out a palm and I looked in that direction to see Monica glowing beautifully in a salmon-pink georgette saree with heavy gold embellishing.

'And today we are meeting, her parents, aunts and I, to finalize Monica's marriage. To Sid.'

It took terrible effort to smile.

'Congratulations!'

Monica beamed happily, a faint shyness in how she lowered her head.

'Can you go and make us tea?' It was worded like a request, but there was a strong element of an order in it somewhere.

'Ask Purnima to show you our special tea set, the one with gold rims and handles. Make seven cups of tea. Purnima will help you with serving the sweets and snacks.'

I looked at Aunty; it slowly dawned on me what she was really telling me. Her smile was sweet. 'And don't drop the tray with my best china on it.'

Now Aunty Karen addressed the others. 'She comes from Hamirpur, Amulya's village. She was left destitute after her father's death, so Amulya brought her here to stay. We are doing the best we can for the poor thing.'

'That's so noble of you!'

'So does she help you with all the housework?'

'No, we still rely on our old servants for everything. They are trained and know the city's ways. But she could learn too.'

Aunty Karen reminded me gently in spite of her impatience. 'Why are you still here? Go prepare the tea.'

I was almost disoriented when I entered the kitchen. But I pulled myself together. Suddenly, all the animosity began to make sense. Destitute, from a village, dependent on Amulya Uncle now—all these traits made me so subhuman in the rigid hierarchies of social acceptability. Purnima and Janani who worked in the kitchen were a little surprised when I informed them I needed to make tea for the guests. Though, I did sometimes brew a cup of tea for a family member when requested. Now, I tried to make it sound uneventful and asked them to help out with the snacks and sweets. I prepared the tea and tasted a spoonful for the sugar before straining it into the seven cups, as requested.

It was with utmost care that I carried the tray in and served all the guests their tea, and finally, handed Aunty Karen her cup.

'Would there be anything else, Madam?'

She gave me a sharp look but did sit up regally to instruct me. 'No, but come back in ten minutes to collect the cups.'

The next time I came, both aunties, Parul and Shubhra, were in the drawing room. Aunty Parul looked up at me, something unhappy in her gaze.

'Come sit, Disha.'

'I...I had just come to collect the teacups.'

'Why? Where are Biren and Sadhan?'

'It's okay. I'll put them away. These are the special ones.'

I collected all the tea things and stacked them carefully on the enormous tray. Only one cup was still being used, by this young man in their party. He gulped his tea hastily to hold it out to me as I waited. And then, he stared at me.

'Hey, I know you. You are Disha from Derozio Dreams. I didn't know you lived with Sid.'

I hurriedly took his cup and left the room.

27

When the Music is Over

*P*erhaps it was a foreboding. Dinner that night was unusually quiet despite everyone being present. Finally, towards the end of the meal, a preoccupied Amulya Uncle broke the silence. And it was by addressing me. 'Have you heard from your sister, Deepa?'

She rarely called. If we spoke, it was only when I called.

'Not lately, Uncle. She keeps very busy. So we speak about once in ten days.'

I hadn't quite begun to wonder why he had asked. 'I had received a call today. She has requested that you be sent to Hamirpur tomorrow.'

It brought a look of instant relief on Aunty Karen's face, but her words, as always, were gracious. 'We'll be sorry to see her go but I guess she'll be most comfortable back in her own place among people like her, people she's known all her life.'

'Did Deepa say for how long?' I asked and immediately regretted it. Uncle looked a little thoughtful. He cleared his throat as he spoke. 'Do you know a young man called Kaustubh? Deepa told me he is her husband's second cousin or something. His family has sent a proposal and they wanted to see you formally tomorrow evening.'

I sat silently, taking in the news.

'If it all works out, your aunt will come and stay with you in your Hamirpur house until the ceremonies are all done. So, in a way you may be leaving us forever.'

I felt surprisingly calm as if I had known all along this was the only logical conclusion to all my misadventures in Kolkata.

'Do you know this boy Kaustubh?' Uncle asked again. I nodded, emerging from my whirlpool of thoughts.

'He's from the village.'

'Is he nice? Do you like him?'

'I don't know him at all. I just saw him around when he was younger.'

Uncle sighed. He was a genial man and perhaps evaded too much thinking. 'I must admit I am a little uneasy. I don't know what the right thing to do is. I don't know whether you should be persuaded into a settled marriage this young. Does Deepa know what she is doing? Yet if I refuse now, what if I cannot offer you an opportunity or a groom as good in the future?'

Uncle looked at me, hopeful of a way out. 'Why don't you tell me what you want?'

'Her sister is her family. She will definitely do what is best for her, even more than you can. Why are you even thinking twice about this?' his wife spoke sharply.

Others joined the discussion, seeming a little unhappy though the words were firm. 'I think it is too early at twenty-one. We can see what happens over the next three years. Disha will have a greater understanding of what she wants to do with her life too. And if needed, we can arrange something then.'

'What is wrong with you all? There is no question of Disha going away to the village to marry some unknown entity.' This was Sid. All eyes turned towards him.

'Don't forget, she has a career, a promising one. We start recording sometime in a couple of weeks for our first album. We have three shows lined up over the next month. A rock talent hunt reality show on TV has asked us to be celebrity judges for their finale. Disha has lot of commitments to keep and goals to accomplish right now for marriage to even be an option.'

An uncle responded to him as he ruminated thoughtfully. 'A career is fine. But she needs a life too.'

'What's wrong with her life?'

Amulya Uncle spoke, 'I am responsible for her well-being, Sid. I can't ignore the realities of Disha's future. She has to be settled just as Lila and Nina were.'

'So she will. In time.'

'In these matters there never is enough time. I can't keep her at home and forget my responsibilities towards her. And I'm answerable to her sister too.'

'I can't see what all this fuss and discussion is about. She has to go,' Aunty Karen pronounced it with an air of finality.

'Disha will not go. She will only go when she wills it, when she wants to. Not when it is convenient to her sister or to Dad.'

'I want to go.' The hovering unease in the room went still. Everyone stared at me.

'Do you know what that means? You may have to marry that Kaustubh.'

I nodded. 'I want to go, Uncle.'

I noticed the tyrannical six were unusually quiet, and even through all this, they had sat without participating, eating in near-perfect silence. Uncle turned to Sid, a trifle unsure, even sad.

'That's it, then. Will you drop Disha to Hamirpur in the morning? I would. But I don't think my back will be able to take seven hours on the road.'

Sid looked cold and withdrawn. 'If she wants to go, let her. I'm damned if I take any part in it!'

'In this household, you have spent the most time with her.'

'Doing what? Struggling to make her fit to be on stage only to be rewarded like this. To have her just leave when it suits her convenience, without a single glance backward.'

'What option does she have, Sid? She may want to settle down too.'

'So let her go and marry the first damn stranger she can find. Why am I supposed to deliver her into his arms?'

'Don't you owe it to her?'

'I owe nobody anything. And it's obvious nobody owes me anything either.'

Finally, Joe was prevailed upon to take me. Sid left the house after dinner. I waited up for the sound of his car to return or his footsteps past my door. I had finished packing. I had few things and it barely took me half an hour. Then, I spent the rest of my time cleaning Lila's room the best I could, hoping it was none the worse for wear after my extended stay in it. It was around eleven when I first called Sid.

He only answered in my fifth attempt, brusquely.

'I have nothing to say to you.'

'Where are you, Sid?'

He didn't answer.

'I was hoping I could say goodbye to you before I leave. Joe wants to leave early, around six thirty in the morning.'

'So you should be sleeping now.'

'I wanted to talk to you, one last time.'

'What is there to talk about?'

'I wanted to thank you, Sid. For all that you've done. I was wondering if I should leave all my stage costumes behind, but they are all so pretty and full of memories, I can't. I hope you don't mind my taking them.'

'What do you imagine I would do with your used clothes?'

'Yes, you are right. And they are awfully pretty too. The best I've ever had. The best anyone could get me.'

If the tone of my voice conveyed anything to him, I wouldn't know. He refused to comment.

'You've turned my life around. No one I know has done so much for me or been so giving.'

'Spare me these speeches.'

'I need to say this. At least once.'

'Save them for someone who cares.'

'Don't you care?'

'No, I don't.'

'I'll never forget you, Sid.'

'Good night. Get some sleep.'

'I love you, Sid. I always will.'

He refused to answer. Tears had begun to roll down my cheeks as I waited for him to say something. But there was more silence until he disconnected the call.

Joe and Jimmy came to drop me. I had hardly slept all night and the silence in the car made me sleepier, until I scrunched down on the back seat and dozed off. I was woken up by Jimmy.

'Disha, wake up. We are stopping for breakfast.'

I woke up far too slowly. 'I don't want any.'

'Eat something. The tea will do you good too,' Joe coaxed me and I followed them reluctantly to a tiny roadside stall.

Deepa was certainly not happy to find me at her marital home in the company of two attractive young men who were not my blood relatives. She was particularly wary of Joe, as if his skin tone alone made his morals suspect. She invited neither of them inside and stopped us just as we were going to step into their huge verandah.

'Who are they?'

'That's Joe...Jatin, Amulya Uncle's son. And this is Jimmy, Jibon,' I corrected myself hastily. 'He is Jatin's cousin.'

I read the look on her face.

'Uncle has a bad back and couldn't drive out. So he requested them to drop me.'

More members of the household streamed out and stood, staring. Joe deposited my bags at the base of the steps.

'Bye then, Disha. Call me if you need anything.'

'That reminds me, Joe. I've left my phone in my...in Lila's cupboard. Please give it to Al. He really admired it. And there's no connectivity in Hamirpur.'

I followed him and Jimmy up to the gate. As they turned to me, I felt the passing away of all that I had come to know and love. I could not hold back my tears.

'Don't cry like this, Disha. Then we can't go,' Joe spoke softly.

I looked at Joe, begging for his understanding, the finality of it all breaking me.

'Is there anything you want me to tell Sid?'

I shook my head, hoping no one behind me could tell I was crying. Jimmy interpreted their stares. 'We simply have to go now, Joe. Bye, Disha.'

And then, he firmly gripped Joe's elbow and led him to the car.

28

November Rain

The tension in the room could be cut with a knife. Deepa was especially jumpy. And by now, I was so numb I may as well have been anaesthetized. In this environment came a little boy barely five or so.

'There is an uncle who wants to see Disha Mashi.'

Uncles did not turn up to meet unmarried mashis in this part of the world. And especially not when Kaustubh and eleven other members of his family were in the process of partaking an awfully lavish spread, being persuaded to make up their minds whether one particular mashi was going to remain unmarried. A tall figure stopped near the doorway to remove his floaters and then bent under the low lintel to take a few steps into the room.

Everyone gaped at him. His cords now completely baggy after hours on the road and his black T-shirt that spelt out 'Nirvana' were patently out of place in this milieu of starched and crisply ironed clothes, decently oiled hair and more particularly of that regulation length civilized men kept.

I stared because in my wildest dreams I hadn't expected to see Sid there.

Sid folded his hands in a namaskar to all the elders before turning to look at me.

'Aren't you ready? I hope you have packed.'

Deepa was now jumpier than a tigress gifted with a full face of porcupine quills.

'Who is he?' she turned to me, her voice an inch from getting shrill.

'This is Siddhant, Amulya Uncle's son.'

'I thought that foreigner was Amulya Uncle's son.'

'Siddhant is his second son. Joe, Jatin, is the third.'

Sid addressed me calmly. 'Haven't you told them yet?'

'Told us what?' Deepa demanded to know.

I shot a look at all the others in the room. Their faces were varying shades of purple and incredulous.

'I am Amulya Babu's son. I am also Disha's fiancé. We are to marry next month. It is what our fathers have wished.'

No one breathed in that room.

'When you called about that proposal of Kaustubh's....' Sid's eyes roved the room and found the right young man as he sat up, desperately trying to reclaim some of the importance he had enjoyed until now. 'Disha decided to come down with my brothers Jatin and Jibon in the morning to inform you herself. And I was to come by later to take her back.'

He turned to me with exaggerated care. 'Shona, have you packed? Go get your stuff.'

The endearment probably rendered unstuck all further questions Deepa was planning to assault him with. I did not need further bidding. I got on my feet and slipped away nimbly. As I turned towards the stairs, I heard all hell break loose in the room I had mercifully just left. When I returned with my bags, the melee silenced as the people turned to glare at me balefully. Deepa looked almost tearful—hopping mad at her plans going awry and being the one left to make lengthy explanations to a horde of furious in-laws.

Sid spoke smiling, seemingly unaware of the awful undercurrents in the room. 'Do you need help with that?'

He now came across the room to where I stood and took both my bags with care. He slung one over his shoulder, lifted the other easily, and his arm wrapped around me, holding me unmistakably close. My eyes flew up to meet his. They most certainly were not smiling, hard and blazing with anger.

※

'Aren't you going to say something?'

'Nothing, except how dearly I wish I could wring your miserable neck.'

The edge in his voice discouraged further attempts at conversation. He drove dangerously fast along the wide deserted roads as night began to fall like long shards of shadows.

'I should probably have just let you be. Your precious Kaustubh and you surely deserve each other.'

'He may have been a very nice man.'

'Too bad you aren't going to be given a chance to find out.'

His voice held sparks of anger and it made sense to remain quiet.

'Do you know what it means to marry someone? You would have to live with him, spend time with him, adjust to all his needs, even sleep with the guy. Had you thought about that?'

'Why is that so tough? I've slept with you, haven't I?'

'And you would merrily go on to the next guy in line, just like that?'

'Then what was I to do, Sid? Never have a life of my own?'

'Why does everyone harp about you having a life? Who was stopping you from living a life of your own?'

'Just let it go. I don't think you'll ever understand.'

'Damn right. I never will. Never want to.'

I turned to the window hoping he wouldn't notice how hurt I was. He didn't seem to care. About an hour later, he wanted to stop at a cluster of shops that spring up alongside highways to cater to travellers.

'I need some tea. What about you?'

I didn't answer. And when he got off the car and came around to help me, I refused to acknowledge his outstretched palm. But I did accompany him to a stone-topped iron table where we sat down side by side on a bench. His phone rang. He looked down at the number as if deciding whether to take it or not, and then he did.

His voice was smiling, intimate. 'Hey, Monica!'

I got up to walk away but he gripped my wrist hard and

forced me to sit beside him as he talked, almost hurting me when I struggled to get free.

'Been expecting my call? Why?'....

'Dinner tonight, at our house? I didn't know...'

'Yeah, I'm on my way back from our village, Hamirpur. I had to come here for some work...'

A lady came and put down two tall glasses of tea and a large plate of pakoras on the table.

Monica seemed to be voluble. Sid slowly let go of my wrist. He finished the rest of his tea in silence and left the money tucked under the untouched plate of fries.

29

Come As You Are

Sid's voice pierced my fog of thoughts. I could sense he was unhappy about something. It was probably me. Or maybe the drive had tired him.

'So you won't talk to me now?'

Leaning forward, he opened the glove compartment on my side and groped for something. When he held it out to me, I didn't take it.

'Where did you find it?'

'In your room. Why did you leave it behind? Were you hoping you'd never have to talk to me or any of us again?'

'It was for Al. You can't use a cell phone in Hamirpur.'

'Do you know how it felt to be in your room and find you gone? Not a trace of you there. Like, you hadn't been there at all.'

He sounded furious. I wondered why he had bothered to come out at all. 'And you call to talk about leaving behind your clothes. Your clothes, damn it! Like I am one of them too, dispensable now that I've been used when you wanted me.'

'At least I called, Sid. You were happy to see me go without even saying goodbye.'

'Why would I want to say goodbye? You are the one who wanted to go. You wanted to give everything up—your home, your family, your music, your bandmates, me. What did you imagine you would do in Hamirpur?'

'How does it matter to you?'

It was pitch dark outside now that the headlights switched off with the engine. Sid sounded resigned.

'You think it doesn't matter, Disha?'

'It really doesn't and you know it. If it did, you would at least try to understand.'

There was a long silence, and then when he spoke, his voice was different, softer and more placatory.

'So make me understand.'

'Just leave me alone, Sid. Everyone will be happier that way.'

'Who isn't happy? You mean Ma? Why should Ma's happiness matter to you more than mine?'

'You, Sid, are just happy as you are. All you need is a woman around—whether it is Monica, Paromita, Annette or any of the countless others whose names I can't recollect.'

'Get out of my car!'

'Now?'

'I mean it.'

My voice held a quaver. I didn't dare open the car door.

'It's dark, Sid.'

'Just get out!'

He was so furious I would probably be safer alone. I didn't need to be told again.

The dread of a thousand creepy crawlies paralysed me as I stepped into the undergrowth just below my side of the car. But bleakness among a torrent of other negative emotions drove me to swiftly scoot into the darkness. I walked, blinded. In a while, I realized there were towering trees at even fifteen-metre spans. I had walked backwards, away from the car, and perhaps stood behind the fifth when I paused to catch my breath and still that panic the unfamiliar darkness caused in me persisted.

I didn't hear Sid drive away. Neither did I try to wonder whether the car still stood there. But everything I had in the world was in that car. I didn't even have my purse. If all Sid intended was to throw me out into the wilderness, he could have just left me to marry Kaustubh. But I recalled how hedged in I had felt in Deepa's extended family's home and how it had seemed alien, stifling. It was with a hot rush of tears that I realized nothing would ever seem the same again.

'Disha, are you there?'

Sid was looking for me in the dark. He seemed to be walking in my direction, calling out at intervals. I stood in silence as he came towards me and then walked past, stopping at almost every tree. I don't know how he saw me in that pitch darkness, but he did. I watched as the blur that was him came closer and stood before me.

'I'm sorry.'

My tears just intensified. The two of us were so

insignificant in the menacing vastness that surrounded us. I wished I had an alternative to having to go with him. I cried harder when I realized I never would. And perhaps he'd never appreciate why.

He took a step closer. 'Please forgive me, Disha. Please say you do.'

I couldn't. I watched in mild horror as he kneeled before me.

'I won't say another word. No explanations. No recriminations. Just come home with me.'

His fingers reached for my hands. Then he held them against each of his eyes for a moment. When he stood up and led me back to the car, I let him. I rested my head against the window, looking at the shapeless blurs of the night flit past.

❧

'We're home.'

I must have dozed off. In the silence of the drive, deeply painful thoughts had taken over. I blinked to dispel their wakeful shadow that hung still. Sid was leaning in and the magnetism that drew me to him was impossibly strong, impossibly bold. My confused thoughts found and clutched at the immovable bars of reality. I willed one to drop between my desires and him now. Turning to find my bag on the other side, I asked casually, 'What time is it?'

A strange sight greeted our eyes. There was a long line of cars streaming down in both directions, shooting off the gates. I didn't recall all the lights being left blazing like this.

As he'd gone past the gates, something made me slow down, a reluctance to step out of the shadows. Or face any questions that could be thrown at me whose answers I'd forgotten to think up in that maelstrom of the ride back. I needn't have bothered. Nobody noticed me.

As Sid reached the bottom of the steps, a female voice exclaimed loudly, 'Ah, so here is Sid! Such an important occasion—why have you come in so late and in such clothes too, may I ask?'

That happy query from Monica's mother did not wait for an answer as she led him by the arm.

'Touch my mother's feet. Our entire family has been waiting for ages to meet you!'

⁂

There was a knock on my door. I hoped it was not who I thought it could be, looking at the door in dismay, conflicted. I felt no need to respond though I still stood rooted in uncertainty.

'Go away, Sid.'

The insistent knocks brooked no alternative. I flung open the door, annoyed at having to capitulate. He looked far less happy.

'Please come down for dinner.'

'I'm not hungry.'

'You have eaten nothing for far too long now. Whatever your issues are, starving yourself is not going to solve it.'

'There are no issues. I'm just tired.'

There was a momentary flash of concern in his eyes. 'Please, Disha. I...' he began and then trailed off. 'Let us, just for tonight...'

Heavily bejewelled and in a sheer magenta saree, Monica looked simply divine and delighted at having found him. 'There you are. I'm famished, Sid. Let's go have dinner now.'

He smiled sparkles at her while the look he threw me was unflinchingly hard. He submitted to his arm being taken, and was led away. I hastily shut the door and went to sit on the bed, spent. The next tap on the door was as unwelcome as the first. Luckily, it was followed by Ranjan Uncle's voice, 'Disha, please let me in.'

He was bearing a light tray and a beaming smile. 'Sid told me you are unwell and some soup was to be brought up to you. All that travelling in one day, maybe. Eat up soon and rest as much as you can.'

*

'Rabindra Sangeet?' Vidyut's voice quavered with disbelief. 'Why Rabindra Sangeet? I thought we had decided it was strictly off limits. And for good reason too. In a city full of expert singers in the genre, it is best for dilettantes not to go there.'

It wasn't often that Sid's suggestions were second guessed. His attention was on tuning his guitar, turning the key the minutest to ascertain the notes were just right.

'It's about broadening horizons and thus reaching a meatier and far wider demographic with our music. It makes sense now that we have a vocalist whose tonality and diction does full justice to the music.'

There was silence. Only Ashraf decided to aid Sid in his efforts with faint plinks on the keyboard of that elusive note he sought to perfect.

'If you mean me, you are wrong,' I ventured. 'Classical training almost automatically negates the requisite tonality you speak of. The two styles are incompatible.'

He had found the note. The strumming now included all the strings and he persisted with tinkering until it sounded perfect. Shady chipped in. 'So, dude, do you have a song in mind?'

'*Amaro porana jaha chay....*'

Someone groaned. Vidyut annotated.

'Not that! It's been overdone, over-sung and over-interpreted to drabness and beyond.'

Sid addressed me. 'Do you know the song?'

I hesitated. I knew Rabindra Sangeet merely as one of the songs I had grown up hearing all around me, barring the handful I had been formally taught at school. This, by some strange quirk, I knew though I couldn't quite recall when I'd last heard it. Sid went ahead to provide the opening bars.

The melody went further into the higher octave than I was comfortable with and he accounted for it by providing me a lower scale. The subtle adjustment permitted me to rove the range with ease. I saw Nishith find a chair, turn and straddle its back to listen more carefully. Transliterated, this was what the lyrics meant.

*What my heart desires
is you, just you
in my world there is none else
nothing else
If peace eludes you
go in search for it
for I have found you deep within my heart
and seek nothing else*

The chorus and the first verse were not the best I'd sung. In fact, that I could belt out a passable version surprised me. Yet, I began to falter as I settled into the mid-scale tones of the second stanza.

*I will lose myself in your absence
will live by your memories
each long day, each long night...*

I couldn't go on. I just couldn't find the song any more. Only then, I realized that the guys had frozen, listening rapt. A beat later, Sid took it up. I didn't know he sang at all. And now, a pleasant baritone sang from where I had left off.

*Long years and months;
if you love someone else...*

For the first time ever during a practice session, I left and escaped to the little sit-out adjoining the room. The garden outside turned blurry to my eyes. By his tread, I knew who had come up behind me. His arms held me lightly and I leaned against the strength he offered.

'Sid tells me you had returned to your village.'

I nodded.

'You can't give up without a fight. You must tell him how it is, Disha. For all you know, he reciprocates but is fighting his own doubts and battles.'

This time, I shook my head wearily.

What would Nishith understand of the whole miserable mess?

'Or you could marry me. That way you could still see Sid for the rest of your life.'

'Idiot!' But he had made me smile.

At that moment, Shady stuck his head into the doorway. 'Vocalists are being requisitioned.'

30

I'm Just a Singer in a Rock and Roll Band

The thing with downward spirals is the undefined bottom. In fact, it is debatable whether there is any bottom or just deeper darker whorls of gloom that stretch into infinity. Sometimes, life affords the luxury of solitude. For more blessed souls, life affords space to lick wounds, willpower to heal and respite from the all-encompassing blackness. Back into the full glare of the household, I had no such reprieve.

I treaded daily on that razor edge of apparent normalcy. The life of an imposter was difficult. While grief froze me within, I had to remain fluid and even convivial at the surface. This evening had provided a sorely needed respite. Left alone with my dark thoughts I was slowly arriving at the conclusion that perhaps pretence was the better alternative.

When the key turned in the lock close to midnight, I expected to see the guys returning from their jaunt to this new hip nightclub strongly recommended by the organizers of the event we were at and other locals. It wasn't. It was

Sid, bedraggled, soaked to his skin. Concern burst out of me. 'Where were you? The guys kept calling.'

He stood dripping at the threshold looking the most lost and uncertain I'd ever seen him. 'I'd gone out for a walk.'

'For three hours? In this weather?'

The queries were probably more than he budgeted for and now he ambled towards the room he shared with Vidyut. These days we hardly ever talked. Each conversation was forced, had an almost abrasive quality.

'Did you get dinner?'

'I'm fine.'

'You didn't, did you?'

He turned at the doorway, hints of the cold rain still in his eyes.

'How was your dinner with Nishith?' he asked.

It didn't make sense.

'The guys wanted to explore this new nightclub in town that was highly recommended. And they kept calling you to join in.' Concern took over again. 'I've just taken a bath in there, I'm sure the water in the geyser is still warm. You need to wash off all the rainwater, Sid.'

I pointed in the direction of the bathroom. He didn't argue.

This apartment we'd been given as accommodation at Durgapur had a working kitchen and I went to see what I could rustle up. It helped that Sid took his time in the bath. When he emerged he saw me set the table.

'Was there food left over?'

'This is cooking in a jiffy that my Baba patented. Of course, I've elevated it to a fine art.'

He didn't seem to share my desire to make the atmosphere lighter. But he did come to sit for his meal as I hurriedly served him. 'Don't have high expectations from the chicken. Baba called it Jungle Chicken—like if you shot a bird while hunting and had the barest of ingredients, a few chillies, onions and a tomato or two? And this is what he would rustle up.'

'Smells good.'

'It's always to be served way beyond mealtimes, when the diner is too hungry to be picky. And it emerges a winner each time!'

A tight smile flashed in my direction.

'With the thunderstorm and all, will there be a concert tomorrow?'

'That's a call the organizers need to take. If there is a postponement—and it is a logistical nightmare if it is—we may have to stay back a couple of days. Anyway, it's like a paid holiday for all of us in the band.'

There was silence while he started on his meal. It felt surreal, this conversation with Sid silent for too long.

I thought back. 'Why did you think I was going to have dinner with Nishith?'

He didn't reply for so long, I began to wonder.

'Nishith and I had a long talk earlier this evening. He wanted my advice about you and needed to clarify some apprehensions he had.'

'Why does Nishith have apprehensions about me?'

'I'm a little unsure really. I think he wants to marry you, Disha, and he wanted me to approve. He needed assurance.'

'What assurance?'

Sid picked his words with care. 'That he wasn't getting in the way. He thought I might mind. He had doubts about Kharagpur. But things like Kharagpur happen. He must get past it all if he wants to start a life with you.'

'Kharagpur' was a euphemism for us—for what had once been my life and its dreams. Something hurt inside me when I heard him speak so casually, almost dismissively, about it all.

'If Nishith asks me to marry him, I think I'll just say yes.'

He stopped eating for a moment and then said, 'I wish you both every happiness.'

'Do you really, Sid?'

Our eyes met briefly. Sid went back to his meal.

'I understand that our lives will diverge, have already, very widely too. But you could still talk to me instead of freezing me out as you have done since you've brought me back from Hamirpur.'

Quite unfairly, that seemed to inflame him. 'You surely did not imagine you could retain a relationship with me, be friends or call sometimes, after you married Kaustubh! Disha, going away the way you did was a choice. And you have every right to make that choice. Only you cannot compel me to accept it and pretend it didn't happen or doesn't matter. Besides, I am talking to you now.'

'Only to tell me to marry Nishith.'

'No, I just verbalized what I think is his probable intention. The decision to marry him is and will be yours.'

The food was forgotten as he looked at the wall opposite him, as if preoccupied with other thoughts.

'Instead of going away to marry Kaustubh or thinking of marrying Nishith or anybody, why can't things remain as they are? Why can't you go on as you've done all along this past year?'

'I do still stay in your house, haven't you noticed?'

'Then why are you in such a hurry to change that?'

'Because things change. That's how things are. I can't live there forever. I must find my own life to lead and my own sources of happiness.'

'A life and happiness are not things someone else will gift you.'

'You wouldn't know. The women that you love do that anyway.'

He looked at me, a fleeting expression of the desire to hide away in his eyes. Very subtly, his tone assumed a hint of determination.

'Ever since your departure for Hamirpur, I have resolved to respect your decisions. I won't argue with you, Disha. I won't point out that there is so much you refuse to understand. Or that each decision you take impacts other lives as well.'

'Are you worried I'd ruin Nishith's life by marrying him?'

'Thanks for making me dinner. I appreciate the trouble you took.'

The concert did happen the next evening. The crowd was enthusiastic and rock mad, singing along. The collective wish by everybody—whether the audience, the organizers or us—was to have the rain blues blown away by music.

For me, this concert marked another chapter in my evolution as a singer as this was the first time I was conscious of a clear bifurcation between what was inside me and what I sang. In that moment, music became a veil, a refuge, another land I visited. As the music wove away into the night and long after it died, it also drained me.

Many people came onstage while the equipment was being dismantled, and for a while, pleasant chatter and a subdued gaiety replaced the pulsating music of the night. It was informal and quite relaxed. I sought Nishith and drew him aside, almost irritably.

'I thought we knew and understood each other perfectly. So what's this weird nonsense now?'

'Sid's spoken to you, I see.'

'And it came as a shock, a rude one. What was the point in discussing any of it with Sid?'

'It's a kind of code among guys. You won't understand. I couldn't speak to you until I had spoken to him.'

I turned away.

'There was another reason I wanted to speak to him.'

I didn't want to be party to a conversation about Sid and I hoped my silence demonstrated that.

Nishith spoke haltingly. 'Sid needs to know you have options. That you have workable alternatives to being around him forever only to be taken for granted, even without the extra pain he takes to ignore you royally as he has lately.'

❧

We started back from Durgapur much later than we had planned to. Ashraf sat at the wheel of Sid's SUV with Shady beside him. I sat in silence in the back seat, a sleeping Sid beside me.

We had been on the road for an hour when I felt I had to ask. 'Why isn't Sid driving today?'

'Let him be, Disha. He's had a bad night.'

'I thought you guys partied all night.'

Shady turned to fill me in. 'Yes we did. Had a blast and overdid things too. Nishith was pissed drunk. And Vidyut was wild. But Sid, he had a bad trip.'

'What's a bad trip?'

'You won't understand unless you experience one. Just let him sleep it off for now.'

Much later, they woke Sid up to offer him tea at a roadside place. He didn't want any. He asked if we had something for fever because by then he had a raging temperature. All I could find was a paracetamol tablet in my bag to give him. Then he rested his head on my lap to sleep, leaving me even more tangled and confused.

31

Waiting for the Sun

'I thought as a sign-off each of you could wind up with a sixty to ninety second byte that is undirected, freeform. It is totally up to you how you'd like to leave your audience. The idea is to reinforce the grainy documentary feel to the entire movie. '

'By byte, do you mean sound bite? Spoken or music?'

'Anything. The choice is yours.'

'Shouldn't we end the film with a performance?'

'Yes, maybe a minute or two long footage from one of your more electric live performances and we go into the rolling credits. But the penultimate set will be a montage of each member of the band communicating.'

Everybody chooses differently. Shady chooses to speak emotionally on his influences. Vidyut uses unlikely objects from around the house to display the infinite scope of percussion possibilities. I know I can do nothing but sing. I choose an almost-extinct form, the tappa. Its very nature is such, replete with tān and swar variations, that only a voice

Waiting for the Sun

at peak preparedness can pull it off. This is in rāg Darbāri and the simple lyrics are a prayer, extolling Him as an omniscient giver of all that we puny humans need to live by.

'Beautiful Disha!' Nishith calls and I look up to smile at him. The acute eye of the camera catches that, and when it is played back, the exquisite woman with haunted eyes whose smile hides more than what it reveals is unrecognizable.

༚

'It's a very different kind of house, Sid. Nothing like what I've ever seen before. Very you!' Juhi breathes it all in, appreciatively.

That Sid has a house is a revelation to me. Which young man with an impressive family home would? That he was and remains an enigma simply heightens the more I discover about him.

We meet late afternoon for the briefest of work consultations regarding the possibility of dubbing for indistinct bits in the film before all of us drive out to this venue.

With the thrill of a project completed, everybody enters the frenzied party mode with enthusiasm. Luckily, the elevated mood means nobody bothers me as I stay on the fringes of the hall, skulking in the relative calm of the kitchen or moving to the garden to catch a breath, only to retreat when succeeding couples seek the luxury of privacy there. Someone from the production team brings me a lime drink and I cautiously nurse it all evening.

It had long been spoken of, the party that was to be thrown on the last day of the shoot and the revels that are envisaged. However, common sense demanded it be moved to the day after the shoot. Sid had volunteered his house as a venue—a house that is the result of all his savings shrewdly invested in affordable real estate at the far-flung outskirts of the city.

After refuelling with forms of nourishment, either liquid or otherwise, there is a sudden resurgence in the desire to dance. The music turns back to a deafening volume and lights are switched off to provide the right atmosphere for uninhabited dancing. When the initial euphoria of celebrations dies down a little, a lull takes over. The evening mellows; it turns more intimate.

'Play something for me, Sid.'

'There's music already,' he counters, smiling.

At Juhi's insistence, the music system is turned off and a guitar is fetched. On the sofa, a place is cleared for Sid. The garden plot outside is reserved for necking couples so I reluctantly join the circle that has formed in the main hall. He spends a minute tuning, his nimble fingers caressing sweetness out of the strings.

And then, inexplicably he plays an ālāp in rāg Hamsadhwani. That he plays now in the Carnatic style is apparent in the more rounded sound of each note and the mathematical precision of the gamakas. The room resonates to an intense devotional instrumental rendition of Muthuswamy Dikshitar's hymn, *vātāpi Ganapathy bhaje aham.* I have never heard him play that or any piece in the Carnatic style so the mastery with which he weaves the melody comes as a surprise.

'Come, Disha.'

He moves almost imperceptibly to make space beside him while simultaneously drawing the sounds out, flattening, stretching the parameters of the notes as he transitions effortlessly to a Hindustani classical approximation of the same notes. It is actually quite simple to pick up the ālāp where he pauses. The silence between us dissolves into eloquence now. Everything that lies within me, unspoken, pours itself into a song. When his nuanced response comes, I want to read an affirmation in it so badly that I do. It spurs me onto more revelation. In none of our previous practice sessions have we ever reached the almost spiritual quality of this communion now. The small crowd around us seems to dissolve. All thoughts dissipate. I venture deeper into where we are, into the recesses—exploring, excavating and extracting unknown parts of me, for him. Only for him! So lost am I that though musically I knew we have run our course, I can't quite stop. Stretching the final few notes into one last plea. Stillness. There is an electric silence in the room no one ventures to break.

Then words of appreciation flow in one by one, soft like a gathering flock of pigeons. In that afterglow, he draws me close and bends to kiss me on the cheek, easy and affectionate. Oblivious to my flush, of discomfort and of a certain inexplicable stab of anger, he smiles.

Finally, I am left alone to re-spool those masses of emotions the music had unravelled.

Untouched by the whirl of happy faces, jokes and laughter, I wrap my cloak of cold misery closer around me. How do people enjoy parties? In the name of all things damned, why do they? It is all so cloyingly superficial—the faux hilarity, the apparent enjoyment, even the tedious small talk in the guise of getting to know one another. Numerous little skits are played out. In a sense, it is a farewell too, and I can see the dread of imminent parting in some of the interactions.

I long for the comfort of seclusion. I long for those bland rooms that served as lonely rest stops while the rest partied. Now that I am thrust into socializing I have no hopes of escape from, how foolish those questions that ate into me all those dim nights seem. Was I consciously segregated? Was all of it an act of protection? Or discrimination? Having been given a taste, I shrink from this cocktail of strangers, drugs and alcohol. As he may have known instinctively.

'Disha, come join us. This conversation is getting really interesting.'

By the time I move to sit just a little outside their widening circle, Juhi seems to have forgotten me and the invitation she has extended—her question to Sid tinkling with curiosity and intimacy.

'And you never saw her again?'

To Sid's credit, he answers after a pause, slightly wary of the probe.

'On the contrary, I see her every day.'

'Really? What does she say?'

Here, inexplicably, he shoots a glance at me before he says, 'Nothing. She has nothing to say to me.'

Absently twirling a lock of hair between two elegant fingers, Juhi ponders over what he says. This inquest is far from over. Only, it changes direction.

'Disha, you would know, wouldn't you? You live in Sid's home and all. Who is this woman he loved so intensely and has left him *this* broken-hearted? I am really curious.'

All expectant eyes turn towards me. And I have nothing—no clue, no magical name to thrill them with.

'I'm sorry. I really don't know. However, I am not sure he is not kidding. For Sid is engaged to be married soon to this woman he's been in a long-term relationship for years now.'

32

Smoke on the Water

I rush towards sanity in the calmness of the gardens. Ahead, at the far edges of this space, I spot Amit and Param, and inexplicably, my feet stall. Amit leans down to first light Param's cigarette and then his own. They stand far too close and the hug begins a little awkwardly. The way they hold each other unravels tales of caring, desire and a hundred unspoken emotions. And then, they kiss with passion so deep I can sense it even in the inadequate moonlight. Two men stealing a kiss is not what our society prepares us for. Yet it is so natural, a delicate extension of their closeness and collaboration. I sense need and hunger; I sense a communion of the souls and marvel at being witness to such sacred togetherness.

That unspoken music between the two directors of our film, is it this? A love neither can express nor hide? Is love always like this—simple and timeless between two hearts, but snarled hopelessly by the intrusion of the world?

'Mind if I join you?'

Idiotic schoolgirl jokes of 'why, am I coming apart?' offer

themselves as responses. I say nothing. He lowers himself on the garden bench, keeping a respectable distance from me. The cold moonlight is just a smoky haze around us.

'Naive of me, you know. I had imagined the party would be all done by midnight.'

Behind us at the house, the revels seem to be picking up deafeningly. Thankfully, there are empty homes, barren fields or plots all around so no one will call the cops.

'Yet another project done. Gets tougher each time.'

He fidgets with the ice in the glass he is drinking from. Sid is exhausted these days; I can fathom. I don't quite understand that palpable sense of despair though.

'When this rockumentary project was first mooted, I was enthusiastic. There were many reasons why it was a good thing.' In the darkness, I know by the relaxation in his voice that he has summoned up a smile. 'And you are a movie star too now, Disha.'

'Movie star? That could not have been why you agreed to the project.'

Sid has a habit of resting his left palm against his right shoulder, forming a sort of protective barrier. But he normally doesn't do this around people, only in moments he is unguarded and alone—sometimes while driving. I assume it is his inner introvert.

'Man proposes. That is all he can do. For things have their own way of not working out as intended.'

'Are you saying the project is not up to your expectations?'

'On that count I have no regrets. Just that everything

else has changed irretrievably. Everything of consequence to me, that is.'

From barely speaking to me to this almost chattiness, the transformation is unwarranted. I don't look at him. I knew Sid's features are inscrutable these days. Mine is an inaudible sigh.

'Why are you really speaking to me now, Sid, when we both know you prefer not to at all?'

The words come like bullets, encased with rage.

'You ask, Disha. If you are unsure about my motives or intentions or any damn thing about me, you ask! You don't risk marrying the first stranger that comes along. You don't stake my future happiness, my very life, on your inability to ask. Or trust.'

His words make no sense. I only gauge anger in them, and disapproval.

Then, I enunciate my awful thoughts in words. 'Don't read too much into what has happened. You know, at Kharagpur... The fact that you have had so many girlfriends in a way reassured me that you would understand.' Here, I need to take a deep gulp of the night air. 'Briefly, all too briefly, I was swayed by proximities. I am not the first girl to lose her head over a rock star or sleep with one. I am aware of how this game plays out. I have nothing to ask. Nor regret.'

'What did you just say?'

I emerge from the shallows of my courage to counter his words and the iced fury of his gaze. 'Consider it a small token of thanks for all the music.'

Night is a symphony of plaintive music—of leaves swishing in small bursts of breeze, in the cadences of a moon skimming past clouds, in stillness and stealth. It has been an ally throughout, through innumerable late-night drives and as the glossary our past passions spoke in. Now it seems to have stopped in its tracks, breath bated, with yet another question.

As if his bones are creaking and old, he gets up to his feet with difficulty. His voice sounds even more aged.

'Come let me show you to your room.'

The stairs are at the side of the house that thankfully enable me to bypass the raucous revels. The room stands on the bare grey terrace, its curtains glowing dimly.

He bends to unlock the door, his words too casual. 'The formal marriage ceremony will likely be in a temple mid next week. I waited out this month for our shooting schedule for the film to be over.'

One step forward and I stop short at the unexpected luxury of the room—despite the palette of inventive green this is a delicate space most suited for a woman. I can't quite place what makes it so for there are no frills or excesses. Still looking around in wonder, I forage for the right words.

'Congrats! I am sure Monica will be very pleased.'

I was spun around to face a rather unreadable expression.

'Maybe she will. However, the bride is you. I was not joking when I told your sister that. To me, it was never a game. And whatever made you "sway", you better hold on to for it needs to last at least one lifetime now.'

It makes no sense at all. I struggle to do the math and finally ask. 'And whom have you decided that I should marry?'

He says 'guess' even as his mouth closes on mine and nothing matters for a while. Minds are very powerful entities, and most often, their diktats are absolute. Trained to be subservient and waiting to be led, the body follows, except when its own desires become compulsions. Despite knowing Sid as a toxin my life cannot withstand, the delight of his lips takes my breath away and makes me relax in his firm arms. Firmer, they circle around me.

'I just wanted you to know why you should only ever consider marrying me.'

Blindly, I turn away and end up facing a bunch of framed photographs along the wall. By the beige and green scarf in a photo, I know that this is from our first concert. This is the largest picture, almost the size of a poster, of me singing. All the others are of me too, and narcissistic like all of us become in the presence of mirrors and portraits, I leave all else to scrutinize each photo.

'Didn't we share a comfort level at least where you could talk to me or clarify your doubts about me and my intentions?'

'What doubts? I knew Monica was your long-term girlfriend. And when I saw her, saw you together at Nina's wedding, I knew how perfectly matched you two were in every way.'

He still studies the portrait, his throat an arc disrupted by his rather prominent Adam's apple as he looks up intently.

'You know me well enough by now, Disha. If I really

had a girlfriend, long-term or otherwise, would I be able to live away from her?'

'I don't know, Sid.'

'Have I been able to live away from you?'

I wonder what all these pictures of me are doing in his room. I wonder what he is telling me.

'Of course. The reason why we are speaking now is that by the rarest of chances I had come to live in your house. You, Sid, are a superstar. Your life, its trajectory, all of it has no place for someone like me; it bypasses me completely.'

His gaze never leaves the picture, seeing something I couldn't.

'How can you not know how much I love you, Disha? Though god knows what these words mean to you. It is probably just like "I love you, Sid, and bye, I'm off to marry Kaustubh." And when I say it or demonstrate it to you, it means I really want to marry Monica and until then I'll settle for whatever happens between us.'

Why is he saying all of which must never be enunciated? These things are best ignored. My voice is tight and small. 'But you are marrying Monica too. A bunch of other women and I were told so at Nina's wedding. Besides I served tea and sweets at the finalization of your marriage talks.'

He grips my shoulders so tightly that the tips of his fingers dig into me.

'Is that what your dash to Hamirpur was all about? And at no point did you feel committed enough to either of us and what we had. You didn't ask what I had been doing with you all along then. Why? Because I'm just such a bastard that explanations are futile?'

All the times I had thought Sid had been angry was nothing compared to what he is now. And all I can dredge up as response seems faint. Yet, I have one clear question.

'Why does your room have pictures of me?'

'It isn't my room. This is your house, Disha. I'm hoping you'll be charitable enough to give me refuge. In your life too.'

I take half a step that brings me close to his chest, a destination that has always been a haven.

'Why are you saying tonight what you've never said before?'

'I did. In everything that has ever been between us. In the language of music.'

Acknowledgements

Despite many hiccups, Bangalore has kept alive the culture of live music. Countless people keep the flame burning. Some by being the best musicians they can be. Thanks to all who work tirelessly to enable this. And special thanks to B Flat, my go-to place for the best music on offer.

Thanks are due to my Bangalore writer-friends who form the most supportive girl gang I know—Andaleeb Wajid, Aruna Nambiar, Jane D'Suza, Shweta Taneja, Zainab Suleiman and Milan Vohra.

The fine writer of mythology, Madhavi Mahadevan, is my sounding board and wise speaker of sense.

It is my good fortune that the talented Pinaki De creates covers for my books. As usual he has done justice to the soul of my writing.

Thank you, Elina Majumdar, for seeing the beauty in my manuscript. And thank you for the painstaking edits, Aparna Kumar.

Atta Galatta and the lovely folks there, Lakshmi and Subodh Sankar, have my eternal gratitude for being my family and my cheerleaders.

Shinie Antony is an incredible writer and, to me, an even more incredible friend. May our coffee last till the end of our days...

My daughters Rashi and Reeti take away discordant notes and weave music into my life.

Every concert I have been to is in the company of one man, my constant star—Kumar. If I know music, it is for him.